CALL FOR THE BARON

John Creasey
writing as Anthony Morton

Call For The Baron

WALKER AND COMPANY
New York

Call For The Baron

Chapter 1

Call for the Baron

'It isn't that we've lost anything of value,' said Martin Vere. 'It's more irritating than worrying, but as it's been going on for a fortnight or more we feel something ought to be done about it. Diana thought of asking you,' he added. 'She doesn't like the idea of going to the police. If you would come down for a few days we'd appreciate it a lot, John. Why don't you bring Lorna?'

John Mannering, of a height with Vere, but dark and lean where the other was red-haired and heavily built, smiled.

'I'll be delighted to come, Martin. Lorna's busy during the week, I know, but she could join me for the weekend.'

'Excellent, excellent!' said Martin Vere. He glanced at his wristwatch. 'I don't like rushing off, old man, but I really want to get back tonight and I'll only just manage the seven-thirty from Waterloo.' He stepped towards the door, adding as Mannering opened it: 'Let me know what train you're catching, and I'll have you met.'

They shook hands, and Vere went out quickly. Mannering smiled as he watched from the window of his flat, seeing Vere climb into a taxi waiting in Brook Street.

In appearance Vere was no older than when Mannering had first known him, ten years before, and he remained as naïvely eager to get back to his Hampshire home, and Diana, his wife. He was a Professor of Economics whose theories, frequently scoffed at, were often remarkably sound. An unworldly man. Diana, his wife, guided him gently but firmly in all practical things.

Mannering took a cold shower and dressed quickly. When

7

the front door bell rang he was ready to greet Lorna Fauntley, the girl whom he had been in love with for five years.

She stood smiling at him for a moment, her evening wrap throwing her tall figure into splendid relief. There were those who claimed that she was too heavy of feature to be called beautiful; they did not know her as Mannering did, had no idea of the radiance of a smile that was often transforming.

'So you're actually ready on time,' Lorna said.

'To the minute,' said Mannering. 'Darling, I've news. The impossible has happened: I've a job.'

There was a touch of bitterness in his voice, and the sombre expression in his hazel eyes sent the smile from Lorna's lips.

'A commission, John?'

'Of sorts,' said Mannering sardonically. He offered cigarettes, and she took one. 'Martin Vere looked in,' he went on as he struck a match and she lowered her head towards it. 'There's been a series of minor thefts at Vere House, and Diana seems to think I can handle the bother more discreetly than the police. Diana, in fact, calls for the Baron, little though she knows it.'

'Oh,' said Lorna, slowly, 'I see.'

Four times in the past two years John Mannering had figured in crime sensations, helping the police to trace jewel thieves who had grown desperate and resorted to murder to try to save themselves. The world knew about that, and the Press had helped to build for Mannering a reputation as an amateur detective whose methods differed from those of the police, but were at least as effective.

But there were things that the world did not know.

Lorna did, with some of the higher officials at Scotland Yard. That John Mannering, man-about-town, *dilettante* and social lion, had a soubriquet about which there had grown a legend. The exploits of the Baron, cracksman extraordinary, had captured the imagination of the people of two continents. There had been times when the Press had given voice to a scarcely veiled admiration, and when the

Baron had been called a modern Robin Hood.

Lorna knew more: of the bitterness which had turned Mannering amoral for a time, had set him pitting his wits against the police, perfecting cracksmanship and adding to it daring and resource which had enabled him to escape the consequences of his jewel-robberies and maintain his separate social existence as John Mannering. The police had learned of his identity but had failed to find proof. Their efforts had slackened when it had grown obvious that the Baron had stopped working for gain and was concentrating his activities on the pursuit of criminals who had evaded the law.

Yet whenever he was working he took risks, rendering himself vulnerable to the police as well as to the thieves. During those spells of intense activity Lorna had known suspense and fear; and yet had realised that danger held a fascination for Mannering he could rarely resist.

Memory of the anxieties of the past was in her mind now. She had known a chase start as mildly as this call from Vere, yet grow within a few days into a life-and-death struggle with Mannering working entirely on his own, risking everything. It was as if he took those risks for others as a retribution for the days when he had worked for personal gain.

That was not all that was in her mind.

Since the outbreak of war Mannering had tried unsuccessfully to obtain a commission. His first application had been turned down with unnecessary brusqueness, and although he knew of a dozen others who had received the same kind of off-hand treatment, it had not prevented him from feeling bitter because of it. He accepted an insignificant post in a government department, but resigned when he found that there was little to do. He disliked doing nothing: he refused to be paid for it.

Lorna had wondered how long it would be before he found idleness unbearable. Now she did not know whether to be pleased or sorry that Vere had asked him to inquire into the trouble at Vere House. It would provide an outlet for his restlessness, but would it go further?

'You're going, of course,' she said.

9

'On Monday or Tuesday,' said Mannering, his expression gaining a certain animation. 'There are points of interest, darling. Do you remember old Jonathan Vere?'

'Martin's father? Very vaguely,' Lorna said.

'The old man had the house modernised fifteen years or so ago, at a time when he had an obsession about burglars,' Mannering told her. 'He had a safe put in practically every room so that any valuables his guests brought remained their responsibility. It seemed to work. Vere told me that there's never been a burglary since. Until now. He doesn't know whether things are being taken by an outsider or someone on the premises. Small things, usually left on a dressing-table or in a drawer.'

'It could be a servant,' Lorna said.

'Ye-es. But Vere is pretty confident of his staff. He's anxious to get to the bottom of it, I gather, because his brother-in-law will be there next weekend. He told me in the strictest confidence, of course.'

'You mean Victor Morency,' Lorna said, and her expression altered. 'So he'll be there! But I thought he was going straight back to the States.'

Mannering shrugged. 'The movements of statesmen get more uncertain every day. Vere was pretty cagey about this visit, but I gathered that he's particularly anxious not to have any petty-thieving while Morency's there. It wouldn't surprise me to find other distinguished guests for the weekend.' Mannering glanced at his watch. 'But it's nearly a quarter to eight, we'll miss that show if we don't hurry.'

They did not miss it, but Lorna found it difficult to keep her mind on the stage and players. She felt a presentiment of trouble, as if she knew that before the week was out Mannering would be plunged into a maelstrom of danger. Had she been asked to explain why, she would have said that she had felt the same before, and that in the past her intuition had not been wrong.

*　　*　　*

From a kiosk in the village of Vere, in Hampshire, a man telephoned to a hotel in London, about the time that Mannering and Lorna took their seats at the theatre. Both he, and the man to whom he was speaking, spoke quietly.

'I can't guarantee anything,' he said, 'but I think it'll be all right. Everything's watched, you needn't worry about that.'

'I don't like the sound of it,' said the man in London. 'What are the people like?'

'A fair crowd,' replied the first speaker. 'About average, I'd say.'

The other's voice grew hard and metallic. 'Keep your attention well on everything, and don't take chances. It must not go wrong.'

He rang off, frowning. His eyes were hard with an expression not far removed from hatred.

CHAPTER 2

The Unpopularity of Lady Usk

'If someone doesn't murder that woman,' said Tommy Armitage heatedly, 'I think I'll have a shot at it myself!' He sat back in a chair opposite John Mannering, easing his collar from his red neck. His fair hair was ruffled, as if he had run an impatient hand through it. 'Well, why don't you say something?'

Mannering smiled as he leaned backwards to reach a bell push.

'You're not in a fit state to listen to anything reasonable,' he said. 'When you've had a drink you'll feel better.'

'Oh, no, I won't,' said Tommy. 'I cool down too quickly, and I want to keep at a fine white heat of temper. Blast the woman,' he added, with feeling, 'but you're always such a cool beggar, Mannering. Nothing seems to put you out. I saw you talking to her for ten minutes this morning, and when you weren't smiling you were laughing. Oh, well,' he added more mildly, 'I suppose it could be worse, and a drink won't be out of place.'

'I fancied not,' said Mannering drily.

'That's another thing,' said Armitage, determined to air as many wrongs as possible. 'You just say whisky and the soda and water come along automatically. I say whisky and have to send back for the water. Not that I mind much about that,' he added. 'There are those born to command, they say, and thank the Lord I'm not one of them. But seriously, I can't stand Lady Usk much longer. I'll be driven crazy. Do you think she was born like that?'

Mannering smiled. 'Conditioned by life, I should say. She grew up in a London tenement with three brothers and two sisters, and her first job was being a kitchen-maid at an East End café. Ten years later she was married to a millionaire, three years later still the millionaire died, and then she married Usk. Poor devil,' added Mannering dispassionately, but he stopped when Ransome, the portly and middle-aged butler, entered with a tray carrying whisky, soda-syphon, and water. 'A mild one for both, Ransome, please.'

'Very good, sir.'

Armitage chuckled as he raised his glass.

'Well, here's to the death of her,' he said, and drank deeply. 'You know, Mannering, you're a queer customer, if you don't mind me saying so.' He settled down further in his chair, crossing one leg over the other. 'You get mixed up in all manner of odd shows, and you know so much about people. I don't suppose there's anyone else in the house who knows what her first job was.'

'Probably others have heard,' said Mannering. He found Armitage amusing in many ways, but considered it likely that he might prove tiresome on long acquaintance.

Armitage took another drink. 'Well it doesn't matter a tinker's cuss anyway. If she'd been born a duchess I wouldn't have liked her any better. "My *dear* Tommy"! Drat and confound the woman, she's an impertinent baggage. How old is she?'

'About forty,' said Mannering.

'Hmm. She's well-preserved, I will say that.' Armitage cocked a contemplative eye at his glass. 'But there you go again, you see, you even know her age. Is there any truth in the rumour that you're a practising crimin-what-d'you-callit-ologist? I mean, do you go around looking at people and finding all about them from the way they shake hands? I noticed you eyeing me the other day, and I had a nasty feeling that you knew what I was thinking about.'

'I was probably thinking that your tie was crooked again,' said Mannering drily. 'No, I don't practise criminology and as far as I know I don't serve any useful purpose. Lady Usk does. She's on this committee and that, and –'

'To hear her talk you wouldn't think a soldier or sailor could boast a pair of socks if it wasn't for her,' said Tommy with feeling, 'and apparently every cigarette smoked in the Forces is distributed through her confounded organisation. And what do you mean,' Tommy went on, 'by saying you don't serve a useful purpose?'

Mannering shrugged his shoulders.

'Hang it, you oughtn't to have any trouble getting a job somewhere,' said Armitage. His glance strayed to the open french window, and the lawns and rose gardens beyond. 'Who's this coming?' He looked apprehensively at Mannering as footsteps neared the window. Mannering smiled.

'It's your *bete noire*, old man. If you want to avoid a meeting you'll have to run.'

'Then I'm running,' said Tommy Armitage promptly. He swallowed the last of his drink and walked swiftly across the drawing-room.

As the door closed a shadow fell across Mannering's head and shoulders, and a woman's high-pitched voice grated on his ears.

'Why, Mr Mannering, all alone? How ungallant of you, with my poor sex so heavily outnumbered! Cecilie, dear, hold the door open for me in case it bangs my foot. That's right, dear, but *do* give me room to get through.'

It was not hard to see what there was in the present Lady Usk to attract first a millionaire and then one of Ireland's peers. On that warm September afternoon it would have been easy to think her thirty-two or three. She was tall and full-figured, and she had been beautiful. Her eyes were fine, a velvety violet fringed with long, natural lashes – the only part of her face which had not been heavily made-up, but she was a woman on whom make-up seemed natural. As she stepped through the open windows, passing a slim, fair-haired girl whose reserved face held an expression of disdain or weariness, Lady Usk held her left hand in front of her, fingers wide-spread. It was a pose that had grown natural, but it also drew attention to the brilliance and size of the diamond rings she was wearing.

As Mannering stood up she nodded majestically. 'I'll sit here, I think, thank you. Cecilie, there's plenty of room on the settee.' She waved her hands, and the sun caught the

14

facets of the diamonds, sending a hundred fires about the room. Until she spoke, she had looked beautiful, eager and youthful. Her voice destroyed the illusion, turning her into the arrogant, domineering creature that her reputation claimed.

'You look cool enough,' Mannering said dutifully.

'Do I?' Lady Usk beamed on him. 'It's nice of you to say so, but I'm afraid you're exaggerating, Mr Mannering. I really do feel the heat something dreadful. Cecilie don't – doesn't – seem to notice it, do you, Cecilie?'

The sun touched the top of the girl's wavy, corn-coloured hair, as she answered.

'It doesn't worry me, no.'

'I've been for a walk,' Lady Usk said quickly. 'Cecilie came with me, she's such a good girl. I can't walk very fast, with my foot so bad – I sprained it, did you know?' She pushed forward a shapely leg, regarding it with no little pride. 'Cecilie didn't mind coming with me, thank goodness, she isn't one of these modern daughters who think that their only interest in life is gadding about. I really don't know what I should do without her, what with this committee and the other, I work my fingers to the bone as it is.' She looked down at the rings, and then deliberately challenged Mannering.

'Mr Mannering, you're an expert on diamonds, aren't you?'

The girl drew a sharp breath, but Mannering did not look at her.

'I wouldn't say that,' he said. 'I'm fond of them, yes.'

'I love them,' breathed Lady Usk. 'I wonder if I dare – yes, I will, I know you won't mind. I had the most wonderful piece of luck, Mr Mannering. The Deverells, you know. They really had to sell something, and I was able to buy their diamonds. I expect you've heard of the Deverell necklace! I really don't think I've ever seen anything so wonderful. It's upstairs now, locked away of course. I don't leave anything lying about. You don't know who you can trust and who you can't these days. Would you have a look at them for me, and give me your real opinion? If I go to a

15

dealer I know he will tell me a lot of lies, you really can't depend on what they say, can you?'

'There are plenty of reputable ones,' said Mannering. He disliked her manner, and he disliked still more the fact that she was boasting of having bought the Deverell necklace, for he knew that it had been an heirloom of the Deverell family for centuries. Tony Deverell would feel badly at the need for selling, but the Deverells had been hit badly by the war, and their finances had been at a low ebb for years.

'Are there?' said Lady Usk, her voice piercingly shrill. '*I* never seem to find them, I'm always being cheated. *Would* you look at them, Mr Mannering?'

'Of course,' said Mannering. 'Whenever you like.'

'That *is* nice of you.' She beamed on him again. 'Not just now, of course, I really must go and have my afternoon rest, so necessary these strenuous days. Shall we say just before dinner? That's settled then. Now don't walk too far, Cecilie.'

The girl said nothing. Mannering stepped across to the door and opened it for Lady Usk, who rested a hand on his arm as she went through and, halfway towards the stairs, turned and waved towards him. Mannering had stayed by the open door for a moment to give the girl an opportunity for going out of the room. But when he turned, she was sitting on the settee, regarding him steadily. Mannering approached her, smiling.

'It is better outside than in, isn't it?'

'That's doubtful,' said Cecilie, slowly. 'And please don't think that because she practically forced you to ask me to go out that you need do it.' She sounded bitter, and her lips curled a little; it spoiled the youthful charm of her features. 'Please sit down, or go out, or – ' She stopped abruptly and looked out of the window. 'Oh, isn't she *unbearable!*'

Mannering offered the girl a cigarette, and saw that her hand was a little unsteady as she accepted one. He said nothing, and she went on more quietly:

'I'm sorry. I shouldn't have said that, of course. But it's getting on my nerves. We saw you sitting alone in here from the other side of the grounds, and she made a bee-line for you while giving me a lecture on the need for settling down.'

Mannering shrugged.

'It's annoying but not unusual,' he said. 'Most women get to that stage sooner or later, but let's clear the air. I am a firmly engaged man, and my fiancée will be here later in the day, so I'm a perfectly safe escort for an hour or two. Romance, in other words, is off. How does that sound?'

She laughed.

'It sounds glorious! With my step-mother the talk never gets beyond money, diamonds, eligible men and war charities, or some ass like Tommy, who thinks – ' She stopped again, abruptly, and Mannering laughed.

'Why not say it? Who thinks he's in love with you.'

'Do you know,' said Cecilie Grey slowly, 'I'm beginning to feel better already. Will you feel too bored if we go for a walk?' She stood up quickly, and Mannering followed her through the rose terraces, to the meadow land which lay beyond Vere House. From the far side of the garden he could hear voices raised in laughter, and caught a glimpse of four white-clad figures on the tennis court.

Mannering did not know what made him look round at the house before going through the gate, but framed against a first-floor window he saw the head and shoulders of Lady Usk. Cecilie asked why he smiled.

'Your mother's delighted,' said Mannering cheerfully. 'We've given her something to think about, anyhow.'

'And talk about,' said Cecilie sharply. 'Would you mind not calling her my mother? She's not, you know.'

'Let's find something else to talk about,' Mannering said. 'I can see she'll become an obsession if you let her.'

'Ye-es,' said Cecilie Grey. 'The trouble is I can never get free from her. I feel she's watching me now – ' She broke off. 'But of course I shouldn't worry you with my troubles.'

'If you really want to unload them,' said Mannering, 'carry on. It might give you more strength to deal with Tommy later.'

Cecilie smiled against her inclination.

'He doesn't worry me, but – do you know, Mr Mannering, she really thinks that she's tremendously popular. It's quite incredible, but she doesn't even realise that Tommy runs away whenever he sees her coming. And yet,' went on Cecilie more slowly, 'sometimes I feel sorry for her. She knows, at least, that her husband hates her.'

Mannering looked up sharply.

'That's strong language, isn't it?'

'I know, but it's true. I shouldn't say this to anyone else,' she added naïvely, 'but I know I can talk to you. She's always putting a face on things, and yet sometimes I think she's frightened.'

'Frightened?'

'It sounds absurd, I know, but I do think so.' There was a refreshing naturalness about Cecilie Grey now that she had shaken off the immediate influence of her step-mother, and Mannering knew that she had needed an outlet for her bitterness. She walked easily, negotiating the rough meadowland without difficulty, and the farther she was from Vere House the more freely she talked. 'She employs a man to watch her, you know. A private detective, who's acting as her chauffeur here. Have you seen him?'

'I don't think so,' said Mannering. 'What agency, do you know?'

'It's called the Woolf Agency or Bureau, I'm not sure which. Logan looks like a prize-fighter' Cecilie laughed. 'If he gives her confidence I suppose he serves some purpose, but I shouldn't like to go far with him at night. I – well, I'm damned,' said Cecilie. 'He's over there now, talking with another man.'

Mannering followed the direction of her gaze. The two men were partly hidden by a hawthorn hedge, but he could see the broad shoulders and thick bull-neck of a man whose back was turned towards them. The second fellow was smaller, and although he was two hundred yards away it was possible to see his thin, narrow features, and the way his lips moved as he talked.

'That's Logan,' said Cecilie. 'She would probably be furious if she knew he was out of the house. She says she hired him to make sure nothing happens to the Deverell necklace, but she was nervous before she bought them. Do you know she carries most of her jewels about with her? But let's forget her,' said Cecilie, as if Mannering had urged the topic of conversation. 'May we talk about you?'

'For what it's worth, yes,' said Mannering.

But although he talked, answering her questions freely, he was thinking of Lady Usk, and her flaunted jewellery.

Since he had arrived, two days before, there had been no further thefts. Diana Vere had gone as far as to say that his very coming had frightened the thief. The actual losses were even more trivial than Martin Vere had intimated: the total value of the trinkets and cash missing being less than twenty pounds.

Mannering felt that he had been asked to come less because of the thefts than because of the possibility of a robbery of greater proportion.

At his suggestion Diana had shown him the rooms with safes. Most of them – including Lady Usk's – were of the combination type. Several were of ordinary key-type, however, and about the key-holes he had noticed slight scratches, suggesting that a pick-lock had been used in an attempt to open them.

He had said nothing to Diana.

He had wondered whether she was afraid that Lady Usk's jewels would be the next to go, for she was a woman much given to adornment, and was usually emblazoned with rings and brooches of considerable value. To Mannering it appeared that Diana was more alarmed than she made out; and he attributed much of her nervousness to the coming visit of her brother, whose European tour had aroused worldwide interest.

She gave him an impression of vague, indefinable anxiety, and Mannering himself had felt an under-current of suspense which he could not properly diagnose.

Cecilie's mention of her step-mother's private detective was his first intimation of the man's presence, and later, in the quiet of his room, before he started to dress for dinner, Mannering found himself thinking of Cecilie's assurance that Lady Usk was frightened.

That might be the explanation of her abruptness, of her

ceaseless talk. If that were so, Cecilie had given him no hint as to the reason, probably because she had no idea of it.

Mannering pushed the thought of Lady Usk from his mind, bathed and dressed, and at half-past seven sent her a message to the effect that if she were free he would be delighted to see the Deverell necklace. Cecilie brought the reply.

'She's all ready for the show,' said Cecilie, her eyes dancing. 'Don't be too hard on her, Mr Mannering. She's as excited as a child about them, and she's taken everything out of the safe and spread it on her dressing-table for effect.'

Mannering smiled.

'I won't be hard, Cecilie, and my first name is John. You're looking far more cheerful.'

'Altogether your responsibility,' said Cecilie laughing, 'I almost wish your fiancée wasn't coming!'

'Now stop flattering me,' said Mannering, 'pleasant though it is to hear, and lead me to the show-place.'

They walked quickly along to Lady Usk's room, and Mannering tapped on the door. A maid opened it. Lady Usk was standing by a dressing-table which had been moved near a window through which the sun was shining, striking sparks from a superb collection of precious stones. The woman had her hand raised as if conscious of her showmanship. She was excited and pleased – and proud. There was no hint of fear in her manner and Mannering wondered whether Cecilie had given her imagination too free a rein.

'I'm *so* glad you've come,' she breathed. 'It's only a part of my little collection, but to so famous a collector as you, *all* I have would seem trivial.'

'I think,' said Mannering slowly, 'that I'm going to be envious before I go, Lady Usk.' He stepped to the table, seeing that the Deverell necklace was in the centre, resting on its black velvet case. On either side were brooches, rings and smaller necklaces of sapphires and emeralds.

Mannering picked up the diamond necklace.

'*Aren't* they delightful?' demanded Lady Usk, and her voice grew shrill. 'I'm the proudest woman in the world to have them, Mr Mannering. You do believe that, don't you?'

'I'm quite sure,' said Mannering. 'Do you mind if I take them closer to the window?' He stepped past her without waiting, and she stayed by the table, watching him as he lifted the diamonds closer to his eyes. His expression did not alter, although, Cecilie thought that his lips tightened.

He stood there fully a minute, with the sun sending sparkles of multi-coloured light from the necklace, and when he turned he was smiling.

'Yes,' he said. 'They're superb, Lady Usk.'

He imagined that he saw an expression of relief cross her features as he spoke, and immediately she picked up an emerald bracelet and handed it to him. He replaced the necklace, and as he did so he wondered whether she had deliberately tried to trick him, or whether she was unaware that the necklace, reputedly so famous, was in fact made of paste.

CHAPTER 3

Guest of Honour

The gong resounded through the house before Mannering went back thoughtfully to his own room. He imagined Lady Usk to be too proud of her possession to show him paste gems, but he was quite sure that he had not seen the original Deverell necklace. The discovery puzzled and intrigued him, and put him in something of a quandary. If Lady Usk did know and wanted to deceive him, it was no business of his; but if she believed they were the real diamonds, should he disabuse her?

Cecilie might be able to help him.

On his right at dinner was Mabel Vere, his host's sister, and on his left a middle-aged woman who paid full attention to her food and wine, and showed an obvious disinclination to talk. As Mabel's chief interest appeared to be centred in a fresh-faced youngster named Menzies at her right-hand, Mannering found ample time to study the party.

It was not distinguished.

There were eleven in all, including the Veres. Martin Vere was talking animatedly enough to a grey-haired, Eton-cropped woman whom Mannering did not know. At the other end of the table Diana Vere was coping with Armitage and the Rector, a distant relation of the Veres. Lady Usk was talking freely to Tommy on one side and an earnest-looking young man called Dryden, a dilettante convinced that he was a poetic genius, on the other.

Mannering knew that most of the party were keyed up in expectation of Morency's visit, but he wondered whether that was the only explanation of the under-current of suspense which he still could not specify. At odd moments he would catch first one, then another of the guests staring at him, only to look away abruptly when they caught his eye.

Was it his imagination?

Could it be that his reputation had been built up to such an extent that they now regarded him as an oddity?

Mannering did not think so. He had the impression that most of them were nervous and on edge, despite the unceasing flow of conversation and the easy laughter. Twice he saw Diana looking at him, and he guessed from her expression that she was conscious of it too.

Diana had married Vere on her first visit to England, and had returned to the States only on occasional holiday trips. They were a happy couple, Mannering believed, although neither was inclined to demonstrativeness. Their lack of pomp explained the fact that although one of the most sought-after men in England was coming to stay with them they had invited others apparently haphazardly, treating such an event as an everyday occurrence.

Thinking this over, Mannering doubted whether it was wholly true.

It was unlikely that there was no political significance in Morency's decision to stay for a weekend in England when it had been generally prophesied that he would fly back to America immediately his round of visits to the capitals of the belligerent countries was finished. Diana always contrived to make her house-parties appear to be chosen thoughtlessly: it was part of the charm of Vere House. But Diana was shrewd, and undoubtedly she had been careful in choosing her guests for Morency's weekend.

Did that explain why most of them were nonentities?

If Diana had aimed to ensure that no one at Vere House was likely to attract outside attention it was easier to understand her anxiety about the petty thieving. To Mannering it seemed likely that she knew that her brother's visit held a greater importance than either she or Vere had intimated, and that she felt it was essential that the mystery should be cleared up before he arrived.

Although it was denied that Morency was on an official visit to Europe, newspapers and – some said – governments believed that the reports he was to take back to the United States would have a considerable bearing on the European war. Thus his movements had been followed keenly. Mannering reflected that Morency might have to keep a firm control on himself if he was to prevent the lionising he had received in all countries from turning his head.

On the other hand if he was anything like Diana, that would not be difficult. Diana, thought Mannering, was one of the loveliest creatures of his acquaintance. He doubted whether anyone had ever known her lose her temper, raise her voice, or show any kind of ill-feeling. There was a charm about Diana Vere which won everyone: he could not remember hearing a word of gossip or scandal against her, which in itself was a rarity.

The conversation at the table lagged.

Mannering wished that Lorna had been able to get to Vere House in time for dinner. He was afraid that she would find driving down from Town in the black-out wearisome, and with the twenty-miles-an-hour limit it might be ten o'clock before she arrived.

The problem presented by the discovery that Lady Usk's vaunted necklace was paste, was still in the forefront of his mind, pushing the original reason for his visit into the background. The more he pondered it the more he was convinced that before the night was out he must make some effort to find whether she knew of the substitution. He glanced across at her, seeing her still deep in conversation with young Dryden. She was saying that she had met Morency in New York and how delighted he would be to see her again.

'And when – ' She turned from Dryden, and raised her voice 'And when, is Mr Morency due, Mr Vere?'

'Eh? Oh, I don't know,' said Vere vaguely. 'Tomorrow, I expect. You never can tell when he'll arrive you know. He always was an absent-minded beggar.'

Mannering lost her next words as Mabel Vere, deciding that it was time she paid him some attention, demanded to know when he thought the war would end.

She would have been plain but for her large blue eyes

which held the attention and partially offset the rest of her features.

'Of course you used to be in all the headlines,' she went on, not waiting for an answer, 'Why aren't you now?'

Mannering laughed. 'It must be because crime is on the down-grade.'

Mabel's eyes turned towards Lady Usk. The necklace was well displayed, and her evening gown, cut low, showed it to advantage.

'There aren't so many jewels to steal, I suppose,' she said, with a bland stare. 'Most people keep them under lock and key. Or sell them,' she added, and Mannering sensed the change in her manner. 'I was awfully sorry to hear that the Deverells' necklace was being sold, when I heard who'd bought it – ugh!'

'That's sheer prejudice,' said Mannering.

'Perhaps it is, but there's something about her that riles me. She – what really does beat me,' added Mabel, dropping her voice to make sure that only Mannering could possibly hear, 'is the display. She's the only one here wearing more than a ring or a small brooch.'

'I'd noticed that,' said Mannering drily. 'But after all, most of you don't wear jewels at all, but prefer to keep them in a vault.'

'Ooooch! That sounded like a touch of bitterness, John. You *haven't* been your real self since you came down, you know. I thought it was because you were missing Lorna, but now I see it's something more than that.'

Mannering raised his brows.

'Perhaps,' he said. 'To be honest I'm tired of doing nothing.'

'That's the detective in you,' said Mabel, 'always on the hunt. Did you know that Tommy Armitage is going round calling you a criminologist?'

Mannering smiled. 'He also told me that I wasn't looking at my best. I'll have to put up a better showing. Does Lady Usk always keep her necklace safely locked away, do you know?'

'Very safely,' said Mabel, and again her smile disappeared

as she looked across at the peeress. 'Diana told me that she virtually invited herself down and then insisted on having a room with a modern safe. Had *I* been Diana I would have turned her out on sight. She's positively asking for trouble.'

'What on earth makes you say that?'

'Oh – I don't know.' Mabel flushed slightly, 'I'm on edge, although I can't think why. Did you know that Lady Usk keeps a private detective?'

'I did – but I'm surprised it's general knowledge.' Mannering was thinking less of what he said than of Mabel's confirmation of the uneasiness: he and Diana were not alone.

Mabel sniffed. 'There'll be nearly as many detectives as guests when Vic comes. Scotland Yard insisted on adding two to his *entourage* – what a word for Vicky! – and then he brought two with him from Washington. And I think he's got four secretaries, and a valet, and – but never mind that. Can you keep a secret?'

'I can try,' said Mannering.

'Well, he's due soon after dinner,' said Mabel, and she leaned back as if preparing to enjoy the sensation. Mannering's expression remained unchanged, and she grimaced. 'I wish you weren't so self-possessed. One day someone will catch you off your guard, and you just won't know what to do. Are you playing bridge tonight?'

He grinned. 'I'm not anxious, but if there's need for me I'll stand in.'

'I don't think we'll want you,' Mabel said. 'Di and Martin won't be playing, and bridge is the one thing where Cecilie's really had her own way: she doesn't like it and won't play. So that leaves enough for two tables. I feel sorry for Cecilie, at times, poor kid.'

'Do you?' said Mannering perfunctorily.

'Yes,' said Mabel mischievously, 'and there's no need to pretend you're not interested. You took her for a *lovely* walk this afternoon, and Cecilie was *quite* a different girl when she returned.' Mabel mimicked Lady Usk's voice, but on a lower key. 'I expect she's poured out all her troubles to you,

John, that's the worst or best of having a reputation for being a – '

'Criminologist,' said Mannering.

'Thank you, sir. People, especially the young and innocent, always think you can put the world right for them,' Mabel went on breezily. 'I remember I told you many tales of woe when I first saw you, but I've learned better now. She's a pet, though, and she's kept on a dreadfully tight leash. I think I'd rather be a poodle. Do you know she hasn't a penny in her own right? Her father left it all to his wife. She's got something, you know. Lady U, I mean,' Mabel finished haphazardly.

'She has a lot of things,' said Mannering drily.

He was not sorry when Diana motioned to Martin, and shepherded the women out of the room. The door closed, and masculine conversation rose with cigar smoke. Vere seemed wrapped up in his own thoughts, and Armitage, Dryden and the affable Rector did most of the talking. Armitage, Mannering knew, was unfit for military service, but Dryden was on leave. The Rector talked of enlisting if the war looked like going on much longer.

No one mentioned Victor Morency.

It was an hour later when two cars drew up outside the main doors of Vere House.

Mannering would have seen nothing of them but for the fact that he had noticed Cecilie slipping out to the garden, and had followed her, hoping for an opportunity for discussing the Deverell necklace. The dimmed headlights of the cars showed her hurrying across the drive. Mannering frowned. That she should have left the over-heated drawing-room for the garden was understandable, but there was no apparent reason for her to be hurrying as if to an appointment, in the darkness and without a torch.

Mannering recalled that each night since he had been at Vere House, Cecilie had been missing after dinner, and had not returned until half-past ten thereabouts. Her steadfast refusal to play bridge had amused him: now he wondered whether a regular rendezvous in the grounds explained her avoidance of the card-room.

27

He forgot Cecilie then.

The light from the hall when the door was opened was very dim, but there was a familiar look about the easy-moving man who stepped from the first car and went into the house. Two other men followed him, and then the cars were driven towards the garage at the back.

Mannering could hardly form an impression of a man in a quick glance, nevertheless he decided that he was going to like Morency. The journey, of course, had been made secretly: and the visit might be over before it was general knowledge that the American had been at Vere House for the weekend.

Mannering turned back towards the french windows. He had a hand on the latch when he heard a cry from the other side of the drive. It was short and sharp, and it came from the direction Cecilie had taken.

Silence, and a hushed darkness, was about him. The wind of the afternoon had died down, and there was only the faintest breeze rustling through the trees. A faint glow of light came from the surrounds of the french windows but apart from that the black-out at Vere House was without fault. It was impossible to see more than the vague outline of trees and hedges, and only that with difficulty.

Mannering had gone out without a torch, and wished that he had been less forgetful. He waited, strained and tense, but hearing nothing more decided that the cry had meant nothing. But before he turned to the window again he heard the scurrying of footsteps over the gravel.

He called quickly: 'Is that you, Cecilie?'

'Who's that?' Her voice came sharply out of the darkness, and she sounded agitated. Now she was nearer he could hear her quick breathing.

'It's John Mannering.'

'Oh. Where are you?'

'Just by the french windows,' he said. 'Haven't you a torch?'

'No,' said Cecilie. 'I forgot it. I only meant to come out for a few seconds. I needed a breath of air, it was so hot inside.' She was so insistent that he doubted the truth of her assurance, and wondered amusedly whether Lady Usk had any idea of these night excursions.

He said quietly: 'Are you all right? I thought I heard you cry out just now.'

'I – I stumbled,' said Cecilie quickly. 'Shall we go in?'

Mannering opened the windows, and she stepped through quickly. She was breathing hard, and her face seemed pale: she had lost the cheerfulness which she had shown before dinner, and clearly she was anxious to get away.

He felt, with sharp concern, that she was nervous, even afraid.

'I'll see you later,' she said. 'I'll be down.'

There was a door leading to a rear passage close by, and Cecilie used it, apparently preferring not to cross the drawing-room, at the other end of which were the Veres and Victor Morency. It was a long room, and the trio did not notice the couple at the far end. Morency was speaking in a pleasant, low-pitched voice.

'I'm tired of dinner parties, Di, and I meant to miss one tonight if I could. How many people have you got here?'

'Not many,' said Diana. 'They're all right, Vicky.'

'Do I know them?' Morency sounded tired.

Diana began to name her guests, while Martin Vere stood with his back to the empty fireplace, staring at the ceiling, Mannering had no desire to break into a family talk, and followed Cecilie. She was out of sight when he reached the front hall, but the cardroom door opposite Mannering was open. Tommy Armitage poked his head through, red-faced and scowling.

'Oi, John. Have you seen her?'

'Who?' asked Mannering reasonably.

'Who else do you call "her"?' growled Tommy. 'She can't even sit for an hour in the middle of a rubber! And talk – does she talk! Lady Usk, of course.'

'I haven't seen her lately,' said Mannering, 'and I'm not going to sit in for her, my son. If I see her I'll hint that you're anxious to meet her.'

'Curse you,' said Armitage bitterly.

Mannering smiled and turned to the stairs, but his expression altered quickly. For the second time that night he heard a sharp, abrupt cry, and this time there was no doubt that it came from a woman. Tommy, still by the door, started. Mannering was halfway up the stairs before he heard the cry again.

'*Oh – oh!*'

'It's *her*,' snapped Tommy Armitage, just behind Mannering. 'Does she have fits or something?'

Mannering hurried up the stairs. To him there had been something in that cry which made facetiousness out of place. It had seemed to mingle pain with fear, and they were not pleasant companions. That it had been Lady Usk's voice there was no doubt, and he turned towards her room.

The door was ajar.

He pushed it open, then paused for a moment. She was on her back with her arms flung over her face, as if to protect her from something she was afraid to see. Through the door of the small room leading off the bedroom Mannering could see the safe.

The door gaped open.

CHAPTER 4

Lady Usk Is Silent

It passed through Mannering's mind that when his chief concern should be for the woman on the floor he had spared her hardly a thought. But as Armitage came in quickly he was able to say:

'Look after her, Tommy. I won't be a moment.'

Armitage obeyed, while Mannering reached the safe, and peered into it. He could see nothing, but to satisfy himself he groped inside with his hand, being careful to avoid touching the sides of the shelves. There was nothing there, and as he turned away and looked about the room he was thinking of the paste necklace, wondering again whether Lady Usk had known the truth about it.

Armitage had lifted her on to the bed. A glance was enough to show Mannering that she was breathing.

Armitage's plump fingers were at her pulse.

'She's all right,' he said. 'She fainted, I suppose. I say, Mannering, this is some game! Morency gets here, and ten minutes or so afterwards we get a burglary. It – Great Scott! It's right up your street, isn't it?'

'Is it?' said Mannering. He felt no interest in Tommy Armitage, and little in Lady Usk. He was aware suddenly of his own position, of the fact that if certain officials at Scotland Yard learned that he had been on the scene of a jewel robbery of some importance they would think immediately of the Baron. He looked at Armitage yet hardly saw the man.

'If you're sure she's all right I'll go down and see Vere,' he said. 'Will you stay here, and keep the door shut until you hear Vere or me outside? We don't want anyone to know about it yet. The less talk the better, especially with Morency here.'

'Count me right in,' said Armitage, 'but break it gently to Martin, won't you? It might be rather a jar.'

Mannering smiled: the thought of Tommy Armitage emphasising the need for tact had its humour. But outside the door Mannering stood for a moment without moving. It was warm, but not warm enough to explain the beads of moisture on his forehead. He went towards the stairs, walking slowly, his face expressionless.

For the time being the robbery would have to be kept silent: neither the Veres nor Morency would want a scandal.

Was their need for secrecy any greater than his?

As he went towards the drawing-room he wondered what the Veres would say or do if they knew they had invited the Baron to investigate the thefts. And he had no alibi.

As he opened the door of the drawing-room it went through his mind that the one way of making sure he was in no way involved was to find who had taken the jewels. The minor complications, particularly the fact that the Deverell 'stones' had been no more than paste, were pushed aside.

Diana Vere was facing him and her brother was sitting back in an easy chair. The first glimpse of a finely chiselled, rather ascetic face was to Mannering pleasing, although he thought Morency looked tired. Martin Vere looked round in surprise.

'Hallo, hallo, John! Come in, and meet our lion, though he's more like a tired lamb at the moment, eh Vic?'

Morency smiled. He was not handsome, but his face had a composure that increased the impression of ascetism.

'Don't get up,' Mannering said as Morency started to rise. 'And don't look at me as if I ought to know better, Di!' He raised one eyebrow towards Diana, *petite*, cool and lovely in her black dinner-gown.

Diana frowned, belying the expression in her eyes.

'Did I look like that? I tried hard to hide it.'

'Now, come!' Martin Vere protested. 'Vic, this is John Mannering – John, Vic prefers to be known as Di's brother for the time being, for obvious reasons.'

'Don't take too much notice of Martin,' said Morency, smiling.

'I know him too well for that,' said Mannering. 'And I butted in because I had to.' He rubbed the back of his head, and then laughed. 'Mabel was telling me at dinner that I'd find myself wordless one of these days, and I'm dangerously close to it now. You're the diplomat of the party, Morency – how would you break the news that there's been a burglary – or perhaps a robbery?'

Morency sat more upright in his chair. Diana's smile disappeared. Vere smoothed his red hair with a hand that was not quite steady.

'What's the difference between a robbery and a burglary?' asked Diana sharply.

Mannering said seriously: 'A burglary means a forced entry, Di. I can't burgle a room I'm known to be in, but I can commit a robbery in it.'

Diana said: 'John, what do you mean?'

'I don't know any more about it than that Lady Usk's safe is wide open and empty, and that she fainted, presumably when she saw it. Tommy is up with her now.'

'Good God!' exclaimed Vere. 'He means it.'

Mannering had an impression that Vere and his wife were not wholly surprised, that they had been expecting something of the kind. Morency was expressionless. Diana stood up slowly.

'So it has happened,' she said.

'What do you mean, Di?' The question came from Morency, but his sister continued to look at Mannering.

'I'd hoped your coming would prevent it, John. We – we should have told you before, of course. One or two attempts have been made to open safes. We've seen the marks on the doors. But from the time you arrived nothing happened, and I'd hoped nothing would.' She looked defeated, and a little forlorn, and Mannering could not find it in his heart to be annoyed. He said quietly:

'It would have made no difference if you had told me. The marks were there for all to see.' He glanced at Morency before he went on – 'is that all?'

33

'Nearly all,' Diana said. 'We can't hold anything back now, Martin, so don't interrupt. John, we're quite sure of the servants, and that leaves the guests. I've told Vic all about it,' she added, 'and explained why I asked you down.'

'I see,' said Mannering slowly. 'And only Lady Usk, Cecilie, Armitage, and Dryden, have been down since the trouble started? That's right, isn't it?'

'Hilda Markham's been here most of the time,' said Vere. 'Mabel comes in and out, you know – but of course it's not Mabel. Damn it, it can't be any of them!' he added sharply.

'It could be any of them,' Mannering said, 'and it could be someone from outside who's forced an entry.' He thought of Logan and the little, thin-faced man, but said nothing of them.

'I'd better go upstairs,' Diana said. 'Does anyone else know?'

'Not yet. I told Tommy to keep the door closed.'

'Thanks,' said Vere. 'I – to tell you the truth, John, I'm thinking more of Vic being here than the robbery. That's as far as I've got yet. Can't work up much sympathy for the Usk woman, but I suppose that will come. How much did she have with her, do you know?'

'Yes,' said Mannering. 'She had more than enough. I was thinking of Morency more than the other business, too,' he added, not altogether truthfully. 'I'm not sure how secret this visit is.'

'As secret as I can make it,' said Morency. He stood up, shrugging his shoulders. 'But if there's a burglary I guess there's nothing to be done about it. The police will be discreet, won't they?'

'You needn't worry about them,' Mannering said. 'It's a question of preventing servants from talking more than worrying about the police. Martin, Lady Usk isn't likely to be satisfied with any attempt to cover it up, even if you wanted to. I'm going to advise you to get in touch with the police at once.'

Vere pushed both hands through his shock of red hair.

'Damn it, there isn't that hurry, is there?'

'I think so,' said Mannering.

'But,' protested Diana, 'you've helped the police in the past, John. An hour or two won't make any difference, and you might be able to discover something quite soon.'

'Yes,' said Mannering slowly. 'That's true up to a point, but if I don't discover anything the police won't like to hear about a delay.'

He wished that he could have urged them otherwise, but it was impossible. For his own sake he had to recommend the police: if they decided against it the onus was not on him.

Morency said easily:

'Why, Mannering, I'll be most grateful if you'll see what you can find.'

'Of course he will,' said Vere. 'He's advising the common-sense course, that's all. He knows we haven't got any common-sense, eh, John? Let's get upstairs and see what there is to see.'

All of them moved towards the door. On none of their faces was there the slightest intimation that anything out of the ordinary had happened. Diana reached Lady Usk's room first. She walked briskly towards Lady Usk's inert form, lying full length on her bed. Her hair was dishevelled, her make-up in need of repair, and her eyes wide open but expressionless.

Tommy gave a helpless gesture.

'She seems struck dumb,' he murmured. 'Don't even know whether she can hear me.'

Vere said impatiently: 'She'll be all right with Di. Let's see what's what, eh John?'

There was little to be seen in the dressing-room, or the bathroom beyond. There was a window, set high in the wall, but too small for a man to get through. The bathroom window was no larger.

As Mannering looked about him he reflected that he had been in a state bordering on panic when he had first seen the empty safe, and he was angry with himself. The past had seemed to envelop him, and in a trice he had been back in the days when he had been hunted by the police, when a false move could have brought disaster, and when every moment he had been on the *qui vive*. He did not want to return to those days, and the fact that he had taken fright so easily was disturbing. It was as if he had lost the complete self-control which he had learned so carefully, and which was still sufficiently obvious to make Tommy Armitage comment on it.

His first thought had been to send for the Veres, and to make sure that no one could say that he had caused any delay. Now that it was done he felt that the fears had been groundless: there was reason enough to believe that he might be able to find out who had forced the safe. That is, if it had been done by someone now in the house, which, as far as it was possible to see at a glance, seemed likely. Certainly neither of the smaller room windows were possible means of entry, and he knew that the larger window was shuttered outside, making at once an effective black-out and a difficult obstacle for a burglar to pass.

'Well, John,' said Vere impatiently. 'Do you always sleuth in silence?'

Mannering shrugged. 'Let's have a look at the bedroom window.'

The others waited for him to go into the larger room. He heard Diana say insistently:

'Now come, Lady Usk, it's not as bad as that. We'll have them back for you in a few hours.'

Mannering saw the peeress's eyes turn towards him. In their velvety depths he saw an expression so akin to horror that for a moment he was startled. Then Tommy Armitage passed between him and the woman, and Vere called: 'Go easy with that blind, Tommy. Black-out, you know.'

'A fig for the black-out,' said Tommy heartily. 'Anyhow, there are shutters outside, aren't there?' He pulled back the curtain, and the dark insides of the shutters faced him. Mannering looked at the catch on the windows. There was no sign of scratching, and it seemed unlikely that entry had been forced that way.

'Nothing doing?' asked Tommy, disappointedly.

'It doesn't look like it,' said Mannering. 'I can't be sure, of course, but it wouldn't surprise me if entry was made through the door. In any case climbing the walls in the black-out, when a torch could be seen for miles, wouldn't be easy. I think we can say the door was used.'

Tommy's plump face was shining.

'I say, that means –'

Martin Vere interrupted him sharply. 'What's the next step, Mannering?'

'I think we should bring Cecilie in to look after her mother,' said Mannering. 'Then I suggest a chat downstairs. But whatever we do mustn't take long, Martin. The jewels might still be in the house.'

'Just what I was going to say,' blurted Armitage.

Mannering put a hand on Armitage's arm.

'Tommy,' he said, 'you've a chance of doing something really serviceable. Will you go downstairs and wait in the porch? If anyone goes out you'll be able to identify them. And if we could get one or two reliable servants to watch the other doors, Martin, I think it would be wise. Failing servants we ought to do it ourselves.'

'Ransome, Fraser and Aston are quite reliable,' said Vere, frowning, 'but there are five doors.'

'The two small ones can be locked, and we can take the keys out,' said Diana from the bedside. 'Don't be obstructive, darling.'

'Didn't think of that,' said Vere. He smiled towards his wife, and started for the door. 'I'll send Cecilie along, then. Impress her with the need for silence and all that, won't you? And then I'll go down and see to the doors. You and Vic go back to the drawing-room, John, will you?'

'Wouldn't it be better to use the study?' asked Diana. 'You won't be disturbed there.'

'Yes, a good idea,' said Vere. He seemed unaware of the fact that his wife was guiding him along the course she wanted him to take. The study was on the other side of the landing, but was in a similar position to Lady Usk's bedroom. Morency sank down in a well-worn leather armchair. He said nothing until he had helped himself to a mild whisky-and-soda, and then to Mannering's surprise, he chuckled.

'I suppose you can't see the funny side, but it is funny,

Mannering. I thought this would be the one place in the world where I could have a quiet weekend, and now this.'

'In your place I'd find it trying,' said Mannering.

Morency shrugged.

'You voted strongly for the police, didn't you?'

'Yes,' said Mannering. He could see that Morency was a little puzzled, and explained casually: 'That was chiefly because of you. Mabel told me that the Yard sent detect – Good God!' he exclaimed, 'I'd forgotten that. You've two extra men with you, haven't you?'

'Why, yes.' Morency stared. 'I'd got so used to thinking they were just following me to make sure I didn't get myself hi-jacked that I forgot they could be useful. Had we better send for them, do you think?'

'I do,' said Mannering. 'But we'll wait for the others first. Do you know their names? Of the Yard men, I mean.'

Morency wrinkled his forehead.

'There's a man named Bennett, I think. Yes, Bennett. Rather a quiet, reserved fellow I thought. The other man is a different type, but I just can't think of his name.'

Mannering felt a tremendous relief. Bennett, he was sure, had never worked against him during the days when he had been the Baron, and of the second, so far nameless, detective he was reasonably hopeful he could assume the same.

He had not long to wait, however, for Diana soon arrived, quickly followed by Martin.

'John, I've just thought of the two detectives who came with Vic!'

'We'd got round to them too,' said Mannering.

'I'll ring for them,' said Diana. There was a gleam in her eyes as she looked at Mannering. 'Well, we'll have shifted the responsibility anyhow. The thing that puzzles me more than anything is Lady Usk.'

'And why?' asked Morency.

'She just won't talk.' Diana looked impatient. 'I don't think there's anything the matter with her at all. She lies there and won't open her lips. Cecilie took control very well, and I've had some tea sent up, but if she's bent on being obstinate there's nothing we can do about it. It was a mis-

38

take to have her down here, Martin.'

'Oh, I don't know,' said Vere gruffly. 'I wasn't thinking of her as much as the kid. Her life's pretty dull, and I thought it would do her good. Instead, she has to dance attendance on that old – oh, never mind,' Vere broke off. 'Usk will be down tomorrow, and he can handle his lady.'

'Yes,' said Diana. 'I don't like her expression, though. She looks – '

She hesitated, and Mannering said quietly:

'Frightened?'

'Yes, I suppose so. Of course, it must have been a shock.'

'Easy enough to understand,' said Morency, 'but what makes you say "frightened", Mannering?'

'She gave me that impression,' said Mannering.

'I fancied she wanted to talk to you,' said Morency. 'Did you notice it?'

'No. But it could be, I suppose. I saw her jewels before dinner.' He wondered whether it would be wise to see the peeress and decided to test the theory. It had unexpected confirmation, however, for the door opened as he touched the handle, and Cecilie entered, looking quiet and self-possessed, but more than a little strained.

'My step-mother wants to see you, John. Would you mind coming?'

CHAPTER 5

The Threat

'No,' said Cecilie, 'she wouldn't say what she wanted, or why it had to be you. But she insisted that no one else was to be in the room. I've got to stay outside.' Cecilie uttered a short, harsh laugh which Mannering found disturbing, but he said nothing. Cecilie stopped by the door as Mannering went in. Lady Usk was reclining on her pillows and her face seemed more natural. Her breathing remained short, however, and in her violet eyes there was the expression which had so startled Mannering.

'This – this is so kind of you.' Her voice was weak, the harshness subdued. He felt overwhelmingly sorry for the woman who leaned forward with a hand outstretched. 'Oh, I wish I'd kept them on, I wish I had!'

'They'll find their way back,' said Mannering reassuringly. 'I don't think you need worry about that.'

'I won't ever see them again,' said Lady Usk dully. 'Don't try to pretend I will, I *know*. But – but I didn't want to see you about that, Mr Mannering. You – you saw them, didn't you?'

'Yes, all of them.'

'I – I mean the diamonds.' She was speaking urgently and her breath was warm against his cheeks. 'You saw them? They were all right, weren't they? You didn't see anything wrong about them? Or – or *did* you?' The last words were spoken in a whisper and she went on with hardly a pause: 'You did, I can tell by your face.'

Mannering said quietly: 'It would be impossible to be sure, Lady Usk, without making a thorough test.'

'But you thought they were fake! Didn't you?'

'I did wonder,' said Mannering.

He would not have been surprised had she turned hysterical. Instead she sank back on her pillows, but her wide, fear-stricken eyes did not leave his. She was afraid. For some seconds she lay there, breathing with apparent difficulty, then her voice came, sharper than before.

'You won't tell?'

'It's no business of mine to give an opinion,' said Mannering. He was filled with curiosity, but even if he tried to find out whether she had deliberately bought the paste necklace, it was unlikely that she would give a truthful answer.

There was something pitiful about her, in the collapse of her youth. She looked fifty, and in her dishevelment he could see the criss-cross lines at the corners of lips and eyes.

'I – I knew you'd be all right,' she muttered. 'I don't trust many people, Mr Mannering. Cecilie's a good girl, but sometimes I think she dislikes me. I'm so afraid' – her clasp tightened – 'They –'

She stopped, and her eyes narrowed cunningly. Mannering imagined that she wished she had not talked so freely. He ignored the 'they', and said reassuringly:

'You've nothing to be frightened about, Lady Usk. It isn't wise to carry so many jewels about with you, perhaps, but they can be well protected.'

'I'm not frightened about *them*!' Her lips twisted with contempt. 'They're all insured, I don't have to worry. It's – Mr Mannering, someone wants to kill me!'

She flung the words out defiantly, as if expecting him to ridicule the suggestion, but in her eyes the fear lingered. Mannering felt that she believed what she said to be the truth. He looked into her face; but he saw instead Tommy Armitage's, and he seemed to hear Armitage's words: '*If someone doesn't murder that woman I think I'll have a shot myself.*' It was the kind of absurdity likely to come from Armitage, of course, but in the light of Lady Usk's assertion, it took on greater significance.

There were times when Cecilie hated the woman. Her husband too, was on bad terms with her. Mannering, in fact, had met no one who liked her.

41

'That's a serious thing to suggest,' he said soberly. 'Are you quite sure it's true?'

'Of course I'm sure! Didn't I get that threat – ' She turned her eyes away from him, but he spoke sharply:

'What threat, Lady Usk?'

'It – it doesn't matter.'

'It matters a great deal,' said Mannering. 'If you think your life is in danger you must try to find out why. If you've had threats, you must find who has made them. Or do you know?' he added quickly.

'No, I don't know!' Her voice rose. 'Mr Mannering, I can trust you, can't I? You – you wouldn't tell anyone else what I tell you, would you? Not even the police?'

Mannering said easily: 'It's not wise to keep things from the police, Lady Usk, but I'll treat anything you tell me in confidence. If I think the police should know I'll advise you. It will be your responsibility if you don't.'

'That's all right, then.' Feverishly she slipped a hand into the neck of her dress, and drew out a small silk purse. Her fingers were trembling as she opened the clasp, took out a folded piece of paper, and pushed it into his hands. 'There! That's it! Ever since I had it I got Logan to look after me, but he can't be here all the time, can he? See – you see what it says?'

Mannering read a pencilled scrawl, difficult to decipher because the paper had been handled so much. There was no heading or signature:

> *You've got a lot to answer for,*
> *my Lady! You won't see another*
> *year in, that's a fact. You*
> *can't buy me off with your lousy*
> *money, neither.*

'You see what it says?' repeated Lady Usk feverishly. 'I got it a month ago, and I'm afraid to go anywhere on my own. I – I don't know who wrote it!' she whispered. 'It's no use asking me. No one would want to kill me, would they? I've done no one any harm, I can swear to that!'

'I'm quite sure,' said Mannering soothingly. 'It's probably someone jealous of your money and position, Lady Usk, someone you knew some time ago perhaps. But if it frightens you, why not tell the police? They'll treat it as confidential.'

She shook her head, 'You don't have to tell me anything about the police, I know them well enough. I haven't told anyone,' she went on, 'but I can't keep it to myself much longer. You won't let me down?'

'Of course not,' said Mannering. 'But how can I help you? Haven't you any idea who sent it? Isn't there any way of finding out who it was?'

'I don't know. I don't know a thing!' She was defiant again, and Mannering found himself growing irritated, even angry. He needed no telling that she knew far more than she admitted: it was even possible that she could name the writer of the message. But she was afraid not only of the threat but of the police. To Mannering that was far more important, for it controlled her actions and it demanded an answer which he would not be able to get easily. *Why* did she fear the police?

There were other questions.

Why had she decided to tell him? Had it been in her mind to show him the message when she had sent for him? Or had it come on the spur of the moment? Had she asked him to see the diamonds because she had wanted to find out whether he spotted the deception, or had it been simply vainglory? And – perhaps the most pertinent question – was her fear of the police due to the fact that the necklace was a fake?

'I can't tell you any more.' Her voice broke harshly across his thoughts, and her fingers released his wrist. 'I could do with a drink – a stiff one.'

'Of course,' Mannering said. 'I'll ring for some whisky.'

'No, don't ring! I don't want a servant to see me like this. Send Cecilie.'

Mannering stepped to the door, pulling it behind him. Cecilie was sitting on a settee some yards along the passage, too far away for her to have heard her step-mother's words. She stood up as Mannering entered the passage, and hurried towards him.

'She'll be all right,' he said reassuringly. 'Slip along to the study, and get some whisky and soda, will you?'

'Oh,' said Cecilie with a touch of bitterness. 'She's all right, then, if she's going to start drinking again. Yes, I'll get it.'

She walked off, leaving Mannering with a new thought. There had been a touch of contempt, too, in the girl's manner, not surprising and yet, that evening, striking a false note.

Mannering turned back into the room. The woman's violet eyes were bright again, and a little feverish, but their expression was cunning. She patted the bed where he had been sitting, and spoke in a husky, confidential whisper.

'Don't take *any* notice of Cecilie, she doesn't like me having a tot now and then. Mr Mannering, you won't tell a soul what I've told you, will you?'

'No,' said Mannering, 'but you'll have the police and others asking questions about the robbery, you know. They'll want to know when you last had the jewels, whether the door was left unlocked, and just what happened. When did you bring the jewels back? Weren't you wearing them at dinner?'

Her lips tightened.

'Yes, I was! But no one else was wearing much, so I thought I'd better put them away. They hadn't been in the safe an hour. I came up to get a handkerchief – and I saw the safe was open! I don't know another thing!'

'Why should you?' asked Mannering. 'Where do you keep the combination of the safe?'

'In my purse.'

'And you don't let it out of your possession?'

'Of course I don't! I set it this morning, and I don't trust anyone to know about it.'

'I see,' said Mannering. 'So that no one could open the safe without getting at the combination in your purse. Have you left it about today?'

Lady Usk's eyes widened and her hands started suddenly to tremble.

'You – you mean it couldn't be opened? It –'

44

'It would take a long time,' said Mannering, 'and with that modern safe it would be almost impossible.'

'I – I thought – ' She stopped again, and then said abruptly: 'I left the purse behind when I went out for a walk with Cecilie. I put it in a drawer and forgot it. I can't help that, can I?'

Mannering was glad when Cecilie came in with a tray and the whisky. That the older woman was lying he was sure. She had been so startled when he had told her the safe was difficult to open. It was as if she had taken it for granted that a knowledge of the combination was not necessary. When she had learned that it was, she had lied about leaving the purse behind: he doubted whether she would leave it for five minutes while it contained both the combination of the safe and the message.

At the root of her contrariness and her abrupt changes of manner he had sensed fear. Fear of something unknown – and of the police.

Mannering left her with Cecilie, glad that the conversation was over, although the one apparent theory to fit the mystery was an unpleasant one.

Unpleasant, and at first sight unlikely, particularly if the peeress was as wealthy as her reputation claimed.

She *could* have substituted the fake necklace for the real ones, staged the burglary, and be intending to claim on the insurance company. The value of the Deverell necklace was at least thirty thousand pounds, and to most people would have provided a strong enough motive. But only a year before, Lady Usk had been written up in the daily press as one of the three women in England worth a million; thirty thousand pounds would not be a stake large enough to make her take risks.

Entering the study, Mannering saw that besides Vere, Diana and Morency, a fourth person, square and thickset stood near the desk. It gave him a shock, for he recognised Detective Sergeant Anderson, of Scotland Yard; a man who knew Mannering and was more than likely to remember the days of the Baron.

'Hello, Anderson,' Mannering said. 'You're on the spot

when you're most needed.'

'Good evening, sir,' said Anderson impassively. 'I would like to have a look at the room, if I may.'

'I don't suppose Mr Vere will raise any objection to that,' said Mannering, 'but I'm afraid you won't get much, Sergeant. You'll find Lady Usk in a poor state for talking, too, but I can give you a little information. She locked her jewels away about an hour before she discovered the loss, and she tells me that she left a purse, with the combination cypher inside, in her room this afternoon. For about an hour as far as she remembers.'

'I see, sir.' Anderson did not seem impressed, and Mannering suspected that the professional's contempt for the amateur accounted for it. 'Is Lady Usk ill?'

'I think she should see a doctor,' Mannering said, 'but I fancy she's suffering more from shock than anything else.'

Diana rang the bell, and gave an order to Ransome to show Sergeant Anderson to Lady Usk's room, and then telephone for Dr Brill.

As the door closed behind them, Vere said bluntly:

'Well, John. Have you been receiving confidences?'

Mannering shrugged. 'More or less. Her story is that she left the purse, with the cypher, in her room. Anyone in the house could have got at it, and by it opened the safe in a few seconds. It isn't going to be easy.'

Morency brushed his hair back from his forehead.

'Did you say "*her story is*"?'

'Yes.' Mannering had wondered which of them would see that point first. Morency was quick.

'Doesn't that suggest,' Morency suggested, 'that she hasn't entirely convinced you?'

'She isn't a convincing woman,' Mannering said, 'and at the moment is verging on hysteria. I'm not so interested in her as in your position, Martin.' He paused before he went on. 'The police will probably advise questioning everyone.' He shrugged. 'After that it isn't likely that you'll be able to stop the story from spreading outside. The fact that Morency is here will be bound to come out. How important is secrecy, Morency?'

The American looked hesitant; he was not an easy man to sum up, Mannering decided.

'I'd like a quiet weekend,' he said at last. 'I'm leaving for home on Tuesday, and while I'm down here I'm seeing some people who would like the interviews kept secret. Government people.' He smiled mechanically. 'Everything considered, I think I should telephone London.' He stood up. 'I'll have to ask all of you to go out while I phone,' he said apologetically. 'Do you mind, Diana?'

It was this request for them to leave him in complete privacy that interested Mannering. It proved that Morency's weekend with his sister was far more than the family re-union Morency had at first implied.

Diana seemed to read Mannering's thoughts.

'Vicky doesn't tell us everything,' she said, 'but we knew he would be meeting two or three people, John. They'll be here as guests, of course, quite unofficially.'

'Of course,' repeated Mannering drily. 'And Vicky isn't the only one who keeps things to himself. But isn't it time we gave the others some thought? Tommy's been out of the card-room for nearly an hour, and that won't make him popular.'

Diana looked anxious. 'Will he be discreet, I wonder? He does talk a lot.'

'There's no need to worry about Armitage,' said Vere. 'He talks, it's true, but it's usually nonsense, and he knows when to keep his mouth shut. Go and smooth down any ruffled feathers, Di, and we'll send Tommy in to do his piece.'

She was out again before they had opened the front door.

'They're all right,' she said relievedly. 'They're teaching Herbert a new form of poker.'

Mannering was glad that the bridge-players had not noticed Tommy's prolonged absences. With the door closed it would have been impossible for them to hear the cries which had attracted him.

He frowned. For the door had been open, and Tommy Armitage had heard: why had not the others?

Mannering shrugged: he did not propose to complain

47

about a lack of curiosity on the part of the bridge-players. Vere had thrown open the front door. The shaded light sent a faint glow into the porch, but there was no sign of Armitage.

'Oh, blast him,' said Vere hotly. They crowded on to the porch more affected by the robbery than they wanted to admit. Vere's voice rose impatiently.

'Tommy, your watch is over, show a leg there!'

There was no reply.

'Drat the man!' exclaimed Vere. He shone a torch from right to left. But they saw nothing, and another call brought no response. Vere laughed, a little uneasily.

'That's a fine watch-dog,' he said. 'D'you suppose some-one came out and Tommy's followed them?'

'It could be,' temporised Mannering. 'We'll stroll down the drive I think. Di, it's too cold for you, you'd far better go in.'

She disappeared, and Mannering and Vere moved forward slowly, hardly visible to each other although the diffused light of the torch shone on stunted bushes, the gravel drive and, beds of autumn flowers.

'Tommy!' Vere raised his voice, and then said uneasily: 'I wish he wouldn't play the fool, John. D'you know, this business is beginning to play Old Harry with my nerves. The last thing we want is fuss and bother with Vic on the premises. Damn all politics.' He had gone a step or two ahead of Mannering, and now dropped back. 'D'you know, I don't trust that Usk woman. D'you think she could have been up to some trick or other?'

'I wouldn't say so without good cause,' Mannering said cautiously. 'And we're looking for Armitage, not reasons for or against Lady Usk. I – Vere!' His voice sharpened. 'Shine the torch to the right.'

Vere obeyed, and as he did so Mannering went towards a dark shape lying on the grass verge. Vere uttered a sharp oath and lumbered after him.

'Good God! It's –'

He stopped, while Mannering looked tensely at the face of Tommy Armitage. The white light gave it a ghastly

48

pallor, and emphasised the ugly wound on his head – a wound from which blood was still oozing.

The same thought sprang into both their minds, and Vere voiced it.

'Is – is he dead?'

Mannering spoke quietly.

'No, he's breathing all right. Give me a hand, Martin. We'd better get him up to his room quickly.' He was easing Armitage's shoulders from the ground while Vere took the legs. Thus burdened they went slowly towards the house.

As they reached the porch, the bright beam of a torch, not covered with the tissue paper that black-out regulations demanded, flashed out on them. The light remained for a second, and then went out; but before it dimmed Mannering had lowered Armitage's shoulders to the porch steps.

'Sorry, Martin. Get Morency to help you.'

Then he started to run towards the spot where the light had shone, hearing muffled footsteps moving away from him as he ran.

CHAPTER 6
Tommy's Story

Whoever was ahead ran easily and with confidence. Mannering was puzzled, for the man – or woman – ahead was running in darkness, taking a chance of cannoning into a tree or shrub. That suggested familiarity with the grounds of Vere House.

The drive was a quarter of a mile long.

Mannering's breath was getting short as he neared the drive gates, and he hoped that the gates would be closed. His quarry would lose valuable seconds opening them, giving him time to catch up, the footsteps came more sharply. The runner had moved to the gravel drive.

Mannering kept to the verge.

Though the torch he was carrying threw light only for a few yards, he caught a glimpse of his quarry at last, seeing a man pulling at the heavy drive gates. Slipping out, a pale face was turned towards Mannering.

Recognition came in a flash.

The features were those of the man who had been talking to Logan, Lady Usk's chauffeur-detective. Mannering had no doubt of it, but the importance of the identification would come later, meanwhile he had to stop the man if it were at all possible.

Would he stop to close the gate, or would he be afraid of losing time?

Mannering saw him pull at the gate, heard him swear as it moved sluggishly – and then the other bent down swiftly, picking something from the ground. Mannering saw his arms go back preparatory to throwing, and then a heavy stone hit him full in the stomach.

He gasped and doubled up. The torch went flying from his fingers, and the light went out. He stood in the utter darkness, the wind knocked out of him, and when at last he was able to straighten up he could hear no sound, and could see nothing.

It was several minutes before he found the torch, and when he picked it up he found that the bulb was broken. Angry at his failure to catch the man, disappointed, and feeling queasy in his stomach, he turned back towards the house. The problems raised by the complications seemed less urgent than his own discomfort.

Welcome light shone ahead of him at last, and he saw that he was no more than fifty yards from the porch as the door opened and closed. He called out:

'Is that you, Martin?'

'Yes.' Vere hurried towards him, Morency close behind.

'What on earth were you up to? I thought you'd gone crazy.'

'I saw the torch-light and wanted to know who was using it,' said Mannering. 'Someone hit Tommy, you know. But he took to throwing stones, and I retired.' He omitted to say that he had recognised his assailant. There was no conscious reason in his mind, but in the past he had often found it useful to keep information to himself until he could assess its full significance. That night facts were too nebulous, and the motive of the attacks too uncertain, for him to know just what the presence of Logan's companion implied.

'It's certainly not so good,' Morency said.

It was easy to understand why he sounded worried. As they opened the front door the dimmed headlights of a car turned into the drive.

The doctor, Mannering imagined, and Vere confirmed it.

He hustled the doctor upstairs, while Mannering and Morency went on to the drawing-room. Diana came in soon afterwards.

'*Now* what's been happening?' she asked, 'You're not hurt badly, John?'

'Not as badly as I might have been,' said Mannering, 'Tommy came off fairly lightly too, Martin says.'

'It's an ugly cut,' said Diana, 'but I don't think it's deep. But how senseless it all seems! Why on earth should anyone want to hit Tommy Armitage over the head?'

'He must have seen someone, and tried to stop them getting away, Di,' Morency said. 'Is he able to talk?'

'Have you ever known him silent?' Diana asked. 'Oh, Vic, why did this have to happen when you came down?'

'What was the result of the London call?' asked Mannering curiously.

Morency shrugged.

'They would like it covered up if it's possible. They're sending a man along from Scotland Yard to avoid calling in the local police.'

Mannering felt his heart turn over, but he showed no change of expression as he asked:

'Did they say who?'

'No,' said Morency. 'A man who specialises in jewel-robbery, I guess. Who is it likely to be?'

'It could be Bristow,' said Mannering.

He wondered what the others would say if they knew of his past encounters with this particular chief inspector. He felt a keen desire to talk, and longed for Lorna to arrive.

She knew how much Bristow knew of the Baron, knew that between the Chief Inspector and Mannering there was a queer association that mingled friendship with suspicion: and she would know that Bristow would want a full account of Mannering's movements – the movements of the man who was acknowledged at the Yard to be the cleverest jewel-thief in the country.

Mannering felt a sharp sense of depression. It was easy to remind himself that this time Bristow could do nothing. He was in the clear. Yet there would be questions and interviews that might easily be disconcerting and even make it difficult to explain Bristow's interest away. He was relieved even when Ransome came in to say that Anderson wanted an interview. Anderson followed on Ransome's heels, his face inscrutable.

'Well, Anderson,' said Morency. 'What can you tell us?'

'Very little, sir. I doubt whether we'll get much from the

room or the safe, it seems to have been wiped clean of prints.' It might have been imagination, but Mannering fancied that the sergeant glanced towards him. 'I think you ought to call in the Hampshire Police, sir.'

'There's no need for that,' said Morency. 'An Inspector is coming from London. This affair must be kept quite secret, Anderson, you know that. Are any of the servants acquainted with it yet?'

'Not to my knowledge, sir. Bennett has been in the servants' hall most of the time, and he will know. Shall I inquire?'

'Do that,' said Morency.

'Very good, sir. And do you think it would be possible to make sure no one goes out tonight without saying why?'

'No one's likely to go out in the black-out,' said Diana quickly.

'I'm afraid the damage has been done,' said Mannering.

Diana looked as if she wished he had not spoken, but to Mannering it was plain that the police must know, and quickly, of the attack on Armitage. Probably it was because he, himself, could so easily come under suspicion that he decided to tell the story without first suggesting it to the others, and running the risk of being enjoined to silence.

Anderson listened impassively to the recital.

'I see, sir,' he responded finally. 'It looks as if the man who attacked Mr Armitage might have been the thief, then.' Anderson was a model of caution, and Mannering admired his attitude. 'I'd like a word with Mr Armitage, sir.'

'The doctor's with him now,' said Diana.

'I'll go up,' said Anderson firmly.

Diana glanced at Mannering asking him to go with Anderson, but without speaking. He nodded and followed the sergeant. Anderson made no protest at his company and they entered Tommy's room together.

Dr Brill was pinning a bandage about Tommy's head. The injured man was sitting in an easy chair, and apart from the pallor of his face seemed little worse for wear.

The doctor finished his job, then bustled off to see his second patient.

Tommy looked at Anderson with some curiosity.

'Detective-Sergeant Anderson of the Yard,' Mannering explained. 'We were lucky he was here, Tommy.'

'Would you mind explaining just what happened, sir?' cut in Anderson.

Tommy pushed at his bandage.

'Well, that's easier said than done.'

'Meaning what, sir?'

'I don't know a lot about it myself,' said Tommy. 'You know what I was doing, and why, I suppose?'

'Yes, sir. You were waiting in the porch in case anyone came out?'

'That's so,' said Tommy.

'And did they?'

'Not to my knowledge,' said Tommy. 'That is, I'd been outside about ten minutes when I saw a torch shining along the drive. It was a pretty powerful beam, I can tell you.'

'Yes, sir,' said Anderson patiently. 'That can be dealt with after we have the man. What happened then?'

'Not much,' said Tommy. 'I wondered whether to investigate and then decided I'd better stick to my post. I suppose it was another ten minutes before I heard someone walking furtively, and I slid out to investigate.'

'How far did you follow him, sir?'

'As far as the grass verge, and that was the end for me.'

'I see, sir. Did you glimpse the man at all?'

'Well, I had a vague impression of one of them. A small undersized specimen, I thought.'

Mannering spoke for the first time.

'Was the torch still shining when you were hit, Tommy?'

'Oh, Lord, yes! The beggar behind me must have been able to see me against the light as plain as a whale.'

'Which means,' mused Mannering, 'that there were two of them in the grounds at the same time. They may have been working together, or they may have been independent of each other.'

'Do you have to be a criminologist to get to that?' demanded Tommy, with a grin.

'Now that the situation's grown serious,' said Mannering, 'we'll have it on record that I'm nothing of the kind, but while we're at it, we may as well check what we can, eh sergeant?' He gave the man no time to say 'yes' or 'no', but went on: 'You seemed a little uncertain about your answer when Anderson asked you whether anyone had come out of the front door.'

'Oh, that,' said Armitage, 'Well, I had a vague kind of impression just before I was hit that I saw another light. That dull kind of glow when a door's opened and a shaded light shows. It's possible someone might have come out while I was hunting around for my bang on the head.'

'You can't be any more sure than that?' asked Anderson.

'Fraid not,' said Armitage, regretfully. 'The only thing I can really swear to – and at – is the bang on the head. What do we do next?'

'If you're wise,' said Mannering, 'you go to bed and stay there at least until after breakfast tomorrow. As far as it's possible we're keeping the robbery quiet.' He shrugged. 'An Inspector's coming down from the Yard.'

'A hush-hush affair, eh?' said Armitage with a grin. 'Well, what else can Di expect if she will have distinguished relatives? That all you want, sergeant?'

'Yes, sir, thank you.' Anderson went off, and Mannering felt relief that there was no need for him to concern himself further. It was now a matter for the police.

As the door closed, Armitage looked up ruefully.

'Here's a go,' he said. 'What do you make of it?'

Mannering said dryly: 'If you want a bald opinion, someone in the house stole the jewels and you were in the way of getting them out. One of the couple you saw is probably miles away with them now, and the other comfortably in his or her room.'

'Cheerful, aren't you,' said Armitage.

Mannering laughed. 'You go to sleep, old chap, and let the police do all the worrying.'

'All right, doctor! But for a so-called crime detective, you're showing a deplorable lack of enthusiasm. Determined not to get mixed up in anything where you could get a kick in the pants, I suppose?' Armitage went on. 'Politics and people in high places wouldn't appreciate an amateur. Is that it?'

'We'll say that's it,' agreed Mannering.

He was pondering Armitage's words as he went downstairs. It was like the man to talk nonsense and then to make a shrewd observation that was very near the mark. Mannering smiled a little, and then forgot Armitage as a bell peeled through the house.

CHAPTER 7

Logan to the Fore

Ransome was opening the front door as Mannering came down the stairs. The butler stood aside, and with delight and a stupendous relief, Mannering saw Lorna. He strode towards her.

'You see, I'm practically waiting on the doorstep,' he said laughing. Lorna's eyes lighted up as they gripped hands.

'Hallo, darling! It's been a foul drive.'

'You can't say I didn't warn you,' said Mannering. 'When did you eat?'

'In town, but I don't need more than a snack.'

'I'll bring some sandwiches, Miss,' said Ransome promptly. 'To which room, please?'

'Mine will do,' said Mannering.

He led the way to the drawing-room. It was empty, but a shout of laughter from the card-room suggested that Vere's guests were getting all the fun they wanted out of poker, and also that they had no inkling of the trouble. The longer they were in ignorance the better, although again it passed through Mannering's mind as strange that no one had heard Lady Usk's cry when the door had been opened and Tommy had run up the stairs.

'Where is everyone?' Lorna looked surprised at the empty room.

'Out and about,' said Mannering. 'We'll be able to talk in my room, darling. Many mysterious things have been happening,' he added with a chuckle, but Lorna stopped short and faced him squarely, suddenly unsmiling.

'What do you mean, John?'

'What you're thinking,' said Mannering more soberly.

'I do walk into trouble, don't I? But it won't take long in telling, and we can look for the Veres afterwards.'

Without further speech they went up to his room.

The door shut, Lorna turned and regarded Mannering steadily.

'What's happened, John?'

'The Usk has lost some jewels,' said Mannering.

Lorna gripped the arm of her chair. It was some seconds before she replied, and then:

'Just how did it happen?'

'I – ' began Mannering, and broke off at a tap on the door. Ransome entered, with a plate of sandwiches and coffee on a tray. Mannering waited until he had gone, and then continued:

'There are numerous complications, but the bare facts are that she lost her jewels, including – she wants it to be believed – the Deverell necklace.'

'Oh,' said Lorna, wrinkling her forehead. 'I saw Tony Deverell yesterday. He wasn't too pleased with Lady Usk.'

'Did he say so?'

'Under pressure,' said Lorna. 'Mother or I – I forget which – mentioned the diamonds and then, well, he let himself go. It appears Lady Usk forced him down in price, knowing that he needed the money so badly that he couldn't wait to sell abroad. And now they're stolen,' she added thoughtfully.

Mannering poured her a cup of coffee, talking while he did so. She was a good listener, interrupting only once or twice on a point she wanted clarified. At the end, she said thoughtfully:

'So Bristow is coming down, and there's no way you can avoid him. I wish it hadn't happened, but – well, now that it has, what do you propose to do?'

'At the moment, nothing,' said Mannering. 'If it weren't for a nagging feeling that Diana's worried about something she hasn't talked about yet, I'd wash my hands of the whole business. However – we'll make some kind of progress, and you can help there. Cecilie is sure to talk to you.'

'And what good will that do?'

Mannering said: 'Now listen, Bristow won't run true to form if he doesn't want to know just where I was at the time of the robbery. Until the thief is found, I'm bound to be Possibility Number One on his list. Always provided Bristow doesn't prove that Lady Usk staged the act.'

'That's wishful thinking,' said Lorna. 'It's absurd to think she would try – or need – to swindle an insurance company.'

'Nothing's beyond her,' said Mannering, 'if she's made up her mind to it. But at the moment I'm more interested in the reason for her fears. She *did* have a note. I saw it. Someone threatened her life, there's no doubt of that. How long ago,' he added thoughtfully, 'did she buy the necklace?'

'Five or six weeks.'

'I've not reached the point of "suspecting" anyone yet,' said Mannering easily, 'but it remains a fact that Tommy Armitage voiced the hope that she would be murdered. And Deverell, you say, is nursing a grievance.'

Lorna said slowly: 'He certainly said that he'd like to see her dead.'

'Hmm,' said Mannering, 'a pretty list of suspects.' He stepped to the telephone, but there was some delay before he put through a Marylebone number. Lorna frowned.

'Why are you calling Plender?'

'Because a solicitor is the only man to get what I want easily,' said Mannering, 'and Tony's the only one who won't ask a lot of questions, or charge a fee.' He smiled as he replaced the receiver after being told that there was a ten minutes' delay on London calls. 'It's a pity, darling, it promised to be a good weekend. As it is we've a jewel robbery, *plus* the complications of Morency, plus Diana's secret, or my imagination. We know that there were several men in the grounds tonight, and there's reason to suspect that the chauffeur-detective was in touch with a man who might – I say might – have hit Tommy Armitage. You could call it an interesting set-up, sweet.'

Lorna looked at him narrowly.

'Interesting from whose point of view? I'm beginning to think you're enjoying it.'

'Maybe I am,' Mannering said, his eyes dancing. 'I can

hear Bristow telling me that I'm one of the half-dozen men in England who *could* have opened that combination safe without the numbers.'

Lorna said quietly: 'John, you didn't decide to give Lady Usk a shock, did you? It must have been tempting.'

She broke off, for Mannering's expression had hardened. He gripped her shoulders.

'I almost thought you meant it,' he said lightly. 'But no, darling, I wasn't practising the Baron's old methods. It would simplify matters if I had. And now I think we'd better find the Veres.'

*　　*　　*

The London call came through before they went downstairs. Tony Plender told him that Lady Usk's first husband had left his money to his wife, but half of it – a half represented nearly three-quarters of a million pounds – was tied-up so that on Lady Usk's death it reverted to Cecilie. The older woman, however, had sole right to the interest, although she could not touch that part of the capital.

'No one seems to treat Cecilie too generously,' Lorna said.

'She's reason enough to be bitter,' said Mannering, 'but I think attempts to get her married off worry her more than a shortage of money. Pay particular attention to Diana,' he added as he opened the door. 'I'd like to know whether you get the same impression that I do.'

They found the Veres together in the study. Morency had gone to bed, and Di and Martin were about to go downstairs. They greeted Lorna warmly, and after a few minutes of general conversation, Martin said:

'Er – sorry this has happened to mar your weekend, Lorna, but we're hoping John will get somewhere soon.'

It was a direct challenge, and Mannering smiled.

'I'm not sure that I can, old man. The police will be watching everything carefully, you know, and it isn't easy to move independently. Has Anderson talked to the servants?'

Diana nodded. 'Yes, only two maids were away from the servants' hall at the time of the burglary. Or robbery.' She smiled, but there was no humour in her eyes. 'They were turning the beds down. The rest of them were listening to a Variety broadcast.'

'Your staff only?'

'No, all of them,' said Diana. 'The only one here apart from our staff is Logan, Lady Usk's chauffeur.' She looked at Mannering intently, but his expression was unaltered. 'That's before Vic's people came, of course.'

'Oh, we can rule them out,' Vere said.

'I hope we can,' smiled Mannering. 'Where are the police? I think I'll have a word with them.'

Anderson and Bennett shared a room on the second floor. Mannering found Anderson on his own. The sergeant was friendly enough, although reserved.

'There's one thing I can't miss,' Mannering said. 'If the thief is still in the house, Anderson, we might have more trouble.'

'I've thought of that, sir,' said Anderson worriedly. 'Mr Morency insists that we don't ask for local help, though, and we can't do much. We have to take it in turns to watch Mr Morency's room,' he added. 'I'm just going to bed for a few hours.'

'Isn't there an agency man here?' Mannering said. 'He might be roped in.'

'I shouldn't care to ask for assistance from anyone without full authority, sir,' said Anderson firmly.

'I suppose not,' said Mannering. 'Do you know Logan?'

'Slightly, sir.' Anderson was not disposed to talk, and Mannering soon left him. His chief object was achieved, however. The police were keeping a watch by night, and with one man sleeping and the other on guard outside Morency's door there was no possibility of them extending their activities.

In truth, Mannering saw little need for them to do so, but he wanted to know where he might expect to find them.

Back in his room, he pondered on Logan's position.

The fact that the man had been in the servants' hall with plenty of witnesses, gave him a complete alibi. But Logan would have reasonable access to Lady Usk's room, and if her story of leaving her purse there was true, Logan could have made a copy of the cypher and passed it on to someone else – for instance, the thin-faced man.

There was one objection to that theory.

If Logan and the other had conspired together over the robbery, why had the thin-faced man been in the grounds an hour or more after the jewels had gone?

A tap on the door interrupted him. It was Ransome. Could Mr Mannering spare Mr Vere a few minutes in the study. Mannering nodded and stood up.

'Oh, Ransome – have any of the servants been out tonight?'

'Not to my knowledge, sir, were you thinking of anyone in particular?'

'I thought I heard a car a few minutes ago,' said Mannering.

'That would be Miss Mabel's, sir. Logan had just taken it round to the front of the house for her. He obliged,' added Ransome, discreetly, 'as Mr Vere's chauffeur was – er – engaged. Logan has been playing cards most of the evening, sir, and was glad of a chance to stretch his legs.'

'I see,' said Mannering.

He found Vere and Mabel in the study, Mabel with a cloak over her evening gown.

Vere turned to him at once.

'Oh, John, something Mabel has told me rather – er – struck me as being of interest.' He glanced at his sister's homely face.

'I don't know what all this mystery's about,' she said, looking from one to the other. 'I happened to mention to Martin that I'd seen Lady Usk's man in Winchester once or twice – I've a flat there, you know – and he thought I ought to tell you. What *is* it all about?'

Mannering said easily: 'There have been one or two little thefts, Mabel, since Logan came here.'

'If that's all, why make such a fuss and mystery over it! Well, if it helps, I've seen him go into the White Angel Hotel several times.'

'Could be interesting,' said Mannering thoughtfully. 'Is he driving you back?'

'Oh, Lord, no! I'm going myself – I can't waste petrol on two-way journeys these days. I won't be here tomorrow,' she added, 'but I'll see you on Sunday.'

When she had gone, Vere said quickly:

'It's queer, isn't it, John? The Angel isn't a place a man like that would frequent.'

'Could be,' Mannering shrugged. 'And now I'm going downstairs for a while, old man – don't be surprised if I'm missing for half-an-hour.'

Vere nodded, and Mannering slipped along to his room. He put on a mackintosh and a hat, and changed into rubber-soled shoes. Within five minutes of leaving the study he was in the grounds, but he had left by a side door; at the front Diana, Lorna, and two of the others were seeing Mabel off.

He dismissed a thought that Mabel might be implicated but the news of Logan's movements intrigued him. Logan, he knew, would wait with the car until Mabel took over.

In the faint light from the hall he saw the chauffeur opening the door for Vere's sister. Then the front door closed, and the car moved slowly down the drive.

Logan's footsteps echoed clearly as the man walked without hesitating to the servants' door, which opened and closed behind him.

In the darkness, Mannering smiled wryly. Logan's actions were beyond reproach, and there was little object in staying in the grounds. He did stay for twenty minutes, however, making four complete circuits of the house: he saw nothing to indicate that anyone was outside, and he went back without wasting further time.

The possibility of Bristow coming kept him from making fuller inquiries: it was essential that he did nothing to cause Bristow grounds for suspicion. He was frowning when he entered his room, slipped off his coat and hat, and changed his shoes. Then he opened a dressing-table drawer for a handkerchief.

For a moment he stood staring down, his face quite expressionless, his mind reeling under the unexpectedness of what he saw. Then slowly he put his hand into the drawer and drew out the thing that was lying there – a rope of diamonds, or what looked like diamonds.

The necklace Lady Usk had shown him!

Slowly, his mind still numb from the shock of the discovery, he held the necklace closer to his eyes. There was no doubt that it was the faked one, and that it had been deliberately placed in the drawer as damning evidence against him. His eyes were narrow and the expression on his face was gaunt.

Then, abruptly, came a tap on the door, and its almost simultaneous opening.

He pushed the hand holding the necklace quickly in his pocket, but he was too late to entirely hide it. He had no doubt of this, as he met the apparently startled eyes of Logan.

CHAPTER 8

Visit By Night

Mannering's expression hardened.

'What does this – mean?' His voice was sharp.

'I – I beg pardon, sorr,' Logan had a faint Irish brogue, and his eyes, brown and close-set, avoided Mannering's. 'I thought it was Miss Cecilie's room, sorr.'

'Whoever's room it is, you shouldn't barge in like that,' Mannering said acidly. 'Who are you?'

'Logan, sorr, Lady Usk's chauffeur. Lady Usk sent me to Miss Cecilie's room for some – eau-de-cologne.'

Mannering felt cold with the shock and surprise of the encounter, and the possibilities it presented.

The man's story was reasonable enough, and he was not likely to have invented one which could be disproved by his employer. His eyes had dropped towards Mannering's pocket, as if fascinated. Mannering was acutely conscious of a slight bulge where the diamonds pressed against his side.

His mind was working swiftly now, attuned to an emergency which might lead to disastrous complications: and what he saw of Logan's heavy, ugly face and small eyes he disliked.

He kept his voice sharp and cold.

'I see. Make sure you go to the right room next time, and make equally sure the room is not occupied. All right, you can go.' He struck a match and appeared to pay full attention to lighting his cigarette, but he was observing Logan out of the corner of his eyes.

Slowly Logan backed to the door, Mannering frowned; listening to the sound of his retreating footsteps. Strange that he had heard nothing when Logan had approached.

Mannering slipped into the passage.

He saw Logan go into Cecilie's room. Presently he came out, carrying a small bottle.

He went on to his employer's room without turning round.

One part of the story was true, then; but had Logan really mistaken the room, or had he deliberately aimed to enter Mannering's?

Mannering felt an oppressive warmth as he remembered Logan's quick glance towards his pocket. He hesitated, and then stepped towards the staircase. He was halfway down when Logan returned to the landing and went along a passage leading to the servants' staircase.

Mannering retraced his steps swiftly, deciding to follow the man.

A glass-panelled swing door separated the servants' staircase from the main rooms, Mannering pushed it wide enough open to see the passage beyond.

Logan's footsteps had stopped. Mannering could see only the man's back, when the quiet voice of Ransome startled him.

'Is there anything you want, Mr Logan?'

'I – er – where's a telephone that I can use privately, Mr Ransome?'

'Well –'

'There's a girl I promised to phone,' Logan said confidentially. 'I'll not be wanting all of them downstairs to hear, will I now?'

There was a faintly contemptuous note in the butler's voice as he answered. 'You can use the telephone in my room, if you wish.'

'It's grateful I am,' said Logan heartily, and he walked on.

Mannering hesitated by the door, his heart thumping unpleasantly. Was Logan going to telephone about the encounter? It was probable, and Mannering felt a sickening sense of helplessness. It was past ten o'clock, and it was likely that some of the servants would be in their bedrooms, or on the way to them. It would be risky to follow Logan.

Keyed up to concert pitch, Mannering hurried down to the study.

It was empty.

In the drawing-room he found Lorna, the Veres, the Eton-cropped woman whose name he could not remember, the poet Dryden, and young Menzies. But for Lady Usk, Cecilie, Armitage and Morency, they comprised the house-party, for the others had been there only for the evening.

Lorna's eyes met Mannering's. It was unlikely that the others noticed his tension, but Lorna saw it at a glance.

Vere looked round with a smile as Mannering dropped into a vacant chair beside him.

'I think it's time we moved,' Mannering murmured. 'Will you slip out and tell Ransome to report to you immediately if Logan makes any move to go out?'

Vere could not keep a hint of excitement from his voice.

'I say, John, that's quick work. You don't want anyone but Ransome to know, I suppose?'

'No – definitely not,' said Mannering.

Vere stood up, but before he reached the door Lorna had taken his place.

'What's happened?' she asked.

'A humorist has parked some of the things on me,' Mannering whispered. 'Logan probably saw them. How are you off for petrol?'

'There's plenty in the tank. *Must* you go out?'

'If Logan does, yes,' said Mannering. 'It's in the air, but I think I can keep pace with him. Where's Cecilie?'

'She had a headache, and has gone up to bed.'

'Try to check on that,' said Mannering, with an eye on the door. 'And what do you make of Diana?'

'Obviously there's something on her mind.'

'Yes.' Mannering's brow furrowed. 'There are a lot too many uneasy people here – not excepting me,' he added grimly. He leaned back, and they made a show of paying attention to the poet, who was waving his arms in artistic arcs while quoting Byron. But Dryden finished abruptly, oblivious of the modest applause which followed. Clearly he was affronted.

The Eton-cropped woman joined Mannering and Lorna.

'Shame on you,' she said, and her grey eyes sparkled maliciously. 'You've quite upset poor Mr Dryden.'

As she spoke, Vere re-entered the room. Barely moving his lips, he whispered in Mannering's ear:

'Logan's just had permission to use the car. Ransome's outside.'

Mannering made for the door. He dared lose no time, even at the risk of arousing the curiosity of the others.

Outside, he found Ransome waiting for him.

'Just what did Logan tell you?' he asked hurriedly.

'After telephoning, sir, he told me that a friend in Winchester was ill, and he went to Lady Usk and asked permission to use the car. It was granted,' added Ransome, his lips tightening disapprovingly. 'He is on the way to the garage now.'

'Can you delay him for a few minutes?' Mannering said. Ransome nodded.

'Good. Is the garage door locked?'

'If it is, sir, you'll find the key on the ledge just above it.'

'Right, thanks,' said Mannering.

In his room he donned mackintosh, rubber-soled shoes, and a hat, and then stuffed a dark scarf and several hand-kerchiefs into his pocket. He had been no more than four minutes, but he was on tenterhooks lest Logan had gone too far to be followed.

He hurried downstairs, reaching the grounds by a side door that opened near the garage. The doors were shut when he reached them, and he groped for the key. From the front of the house he could see the glow from the headlights of Lady Usk's Daimler, and hear the murmur of voices. Ransome was excelling himself, but as Mannering opened the garage doors he heard the Daimler's engine start up. Quickly he slipped into the driving seat of Lorna's car and eased it round the house. Once on the drive he spotted the rear light of the Daimler as it turned into the road. Presently he switched off his lights. The glow cast by the Daimler was enough to guide him, and he did not propose to risk Logan seeing the M.G.'s lights in the driving-mirror.

Once on the Winchester road, however, he switched them on again, for there was no longer any danger of being associated with Vere House.

For the first time since Logan had seen him he felt that he dared relax. Winchester was twelve miles away, and at the speed-limit of twenty miles an hour the run would take all of thirty minutes.

But what would be at the end of it?

Mannering had taken it for granted that Logan had reported the glimpse of the necklace, and had received instructions to make a fuller report in person. The one way to learn the results of the development was to overhear Logan's interview. It was vital that Mannering should prevent any word reaching the ears of the police.

If that were impossible, he must find some way of discrediting Logan's story, for Chief Inspector Bristow, or any other man who came from the Yard, would be sceptical of the truth.

CHAPTER 9

The White Angel

As the Daimler reached the High Street in Winchester, there was no more than twenty yards between the two cars. Logan pulled in at a nearby parking place, and climbed out. Mannering looked straight ahead as he passed, but Logan showed no interest in him.

Parking his own car Mannering managed to sight Logan's retreating back just entering the White Angel Hotel.

His pulse quickening, Mannering followed in his wake.

The foyer was empty but for a sleepy-eyed porter behind the reception desk. Mannering spoke abruptly in a voice which few would have recognised as being his own.

'Is there a single room vacant for the night?'

'Yes, sir. Would you like a front room or a back one, sir?'

'I'll take a back room,' Mannering said. He was acutely conscious of his low-pulled hat, and the fact that his collar was hiding part of his face, but he dared not risk letting the man take a clear view of him.

Quickly he filled in his registration, giving the name of Morely, and his last address as the Regal Hotel, London.

'Can you get me a whisky and soda?'

'Why, yes, sir,'

'Then bring me one immediately,' said Mannering. 'I'll find the way up myself.'

'The second floor, sir. Room 9.' Damn the fellow, why was he so attentive? He accompanied Mannering to a lift, giving him precise instructions. 'Turn right when you get out, sir, up three steps, and it's on the left – you can't miss it.'

'Right,' said Mannering, 'thanks.'

He reached his room, his breath coming quickly, his forehead cold and damp. He stepped to the wash-basin, filled it, and was washing his face when the porter came with the whisky and soda. Mannering nodded to a small pile of silver on the dressing-table.

The porter helped himself with alacrity, but still did not go.

'Anything else, sir?'

'I'll ring if there is,' said Mannering from behind the towel, waiting impatiently for the porter to leave both the room and the second floor. Mannering slipped into his coat, pulled his hat once again low over his eyes, and worked on a pair of thin black cotton gloves. That done he left the room.

The passage was flanked by nine doors. Outside seven of them were shoes, evidence that the occupants had retired for the night. He stepped cautiously towards Room 3, the only one beside his own without them.

He put his ear close to the door, but heard nothing.

Had Logan's employer put his shoes out?

From only two rooms came any sound of voices; in each case a woman's. Mannering stepped to the end of the passage. A flight of stairs ran about the lift, and Mannering went down them.

The first floor was similar in layout to the second.

Here two rooms were without shoes: silence came from the first, but as he neared the second he heard the murmur of a man's voice. He stopped, ears alert for any sound of approach from the stairs or the lift; and then he recognised Logan's voice.

'But wid my own eyes I saw it!'

'Don't talk so loudly!' said the second man sharply. The voice was mellow and cultured, and the words were only just audible. 'So you insist on the story?'

Mannering turned the door-knob, very gently. The door yielded a fraction of an inch, and now the voices were much clearer. Logan was saying:

'Well, I've eyes in my head, sorr. And tell me this, why should he be pushing sparklers in his pocket if he had no cause to hide them?'

'I don't pay you to make wild guesses,' said the unknown man suavely. 'I pay you to do as you're told. Did you ever hear that Mr Mannering was a well-known collector of jewels?'

'And if I did?' demanded Logan doggedly. 'Calls himself a bloody 'tec, too, but it don't make him one.'

'That'll do,' said his companion impatiently. 'I thought you'd something of real importance for me. You haven't found Lady Usk's collection?'

'No, but –'

'And all you can tell me is that Mr Mannering was holding some jewels when you went accidentally into his room.'

'Och, yes.' Logan was surly.

'All right. Now what's this about the police?'

Logan's tone altered, and he talked eagerly of the activities of Bennett and Anderson, and of the fact that he believed someone was coming from the Yard on the next day. The man heard him out, and then snapped:

'Keep your eyes and ears open, Logan, and don't do anything foolish. Have you seen Woolf today?' he added sharply.

'Sure an' I did see him, sorr.

'This afternoon as ever was.'

'Not this evening?' There was a hardening in the speaker's voice, and Mannering sensed a sudden increase of tension.

'Woolf has been very foolish,' he went on incisively. 'He was in the grounds tonight when one of the guests was knocked out. You don't know anything about that little incident, do you?' There was a note of menace in the man's voice, and Logan drew in a sharp breath.

'But I never went out!'

'All right. But remember, you'll do nothing without my instructions. Woolf lost his head, and I don't want that to happen to you. Keep that mouth of yours sealed, and report by telephone tomorrow unless you think it's necessary to come here. Make an appointment for that – but make sure it's important enough.'

Quietly Mannering drew the door too. He stepped swiftly to the end of the passage, and was going down the stairs when he heard the door open and close.

Logan's heavy footsteps drew near. Mannering reached the foot of the stairs, and turned towards a room marked 'Lounge'. Logan passed him, going through the foyer to the open road.

Mannering retraced his steps, thinking of that suave, menacing voice.

He reached the door of Number 3 again, and proved that he had been wise to lose no time for he heard the careful voice of a man telephoning.

Again Mannering turned the handle of the door, opening it wide enough to let the words come through clearly.

'Woolf . . . listen carefully – have you heard any rumours at any time about John Mannering . . . what's that? . . . any kind of rumours, you damned fool!' There was a long pause, and then the speaker said abruptly: 'All right. No, I don't want any inquiries made yet. I'll tell you if I do.'

The receiver went down sharply.

Mannering waited tensely. Through his mind passed a summary of all he had heard, and all that it implied. Logan had seen the necklace and had made haste to report it, but his employer had shown no interest until Logan had gone. But the chauffeur's information had impressed him; again Mannering sensed the nearness of danger, and yet could see no way in which he could evade it.

Mannering felt something of the inward excitement of the days when he had worked as the Baron, when an exploit such as this would have been an everyday affair. It was as if a strange psychological change took place in him, as if the Baron and not John Mannering was standing silently outside the door. That he had done nothing to precipitate it made no difference to the issue at stake: a word from the unknown man to Bristow could prove fatal.

Who was the unknown?

The name 'Woolf' had brought a simple explanation of one thing. Presumably he was the owner of the detective agency which Cecilie had mentioned and for which Logan worked. The man at the White Angel either employed the agency and exercised considerable control over it or, using

Woolf as a cover, was its true principal.

Was he working for Lady Usk? Had Logan's call been solely due to the chauffeur's belief that he had found a clue to the robbery? Or was there a deeper motive?

Mannering had to see the unknown, had to find some way of making sure. If the agency was genuine then Logan's report would probably reach the police; but there was far more than the personal issue at stake. There were the other robberies, and the ineffectual efforts to open several safes in Vere House. There was the fact that Morency's visit, although kept so secret, was known to the man here, through Logan; and it *might* have been known before. There was the knowledge that the man who had knocked Armitage out was apparently unconnected with the Woolf Agency; and it was strange that Woolf had thought it necessary to report both that and his own escape from Mannering.

Mannering reasoned that Woolf was the thin-faced man.

There was the mystery of the past two weeks, and the obvious possibilities of Morency's visit to Hampshire. There was the fear of Lady Usk, and the apprehension which Diana felt but had not yet admitted. For all of those things there was an explanation, and the man who had talked with Logan might be able to explain something of them.

Someone, for instance, had sent a menacing, threatening letter to Lady Usk.

Mannering hesitated, not moving.

He could telephone Vere to say that he might not be back that night. He could visit, during the night, Room 3. There would be little difficulty and, he believed, little danger. He would be able to see the man, and perhaps find papers that would give a clue to the other's activities.

If they were strictly lawful Mannering knew the danger could hardly be greater. But there was something furtive about Logan's visit and Woolf's presence in the grounds, lending Mannering a conviction that the activities were not within the law. If he could prove that, he would have a weapon which could be used if Logan's report was followed up, and inquiries grew threatening.

'I'll stay,' Mannering thought. 'And –'

It was then that the door opened.

The man inside had moved so softly that Mannering heard no sound.

He saw a tall, hard-faced man, sallow and thin-featured – with a pair of shoes in his hand.

The man gasped, then stepped back, his right hand lifted with the shoes in them. Mannering knew that they were to be used as missiles. There was nothing for it but to jump forward, his own right fist clenched and raised. As a shoe hurtled towards him he struck out.

The man's knees bent beneath him.

Mannering stepped farther into the room.

As he did so he heard footsteps running up the stairs, and knew that the commotion had raised an alarm. He stooped down swiftly, collected the shoes and put them outside the door, seeing the porter at the end of the passage.

He called in a voice very like his victim's:

'I fell over a chair. No trouble, porter.'

Then he banged the door and leaned against it, breathing heavily and looking down on the man he had felled.

Chapter 10

Alarm!

The porter's footsteps faded. Mannering drew a hand across his forehead, content to relax for a few seconds.

The man at his feet stirred.

Mannering took a clean handkerchief from his pocket, and tied it about the other's mouth then he eased the man up and on to the bed. He used the sash of a dressing gown to bind the wrists.

That finished, Mannering tied his scarf loosely about his own mouth and chin. It would lessen any risk of recognition when the other regained consciousness.

Mannering felt as if the months had rolled back, and he was indeed the Baron again. Tense, alert for the slightest alarm, exhilarated. The difficulties and attendant dangers faded from his mind as he turned from the bed and ran through the drawers of a dressing table. Shirts, socks, collars, enough of everything to suggest that the man proposed to stay for several days, were there; but no papers.

He ran through the other's pockets. The only papers were in a pigskin wallet which Mannering hastily put on the chest of drawers, for at that point the man opened his eyes.

They were grey, so piercing and alert that Mannering suspected he had been conscious for some minutes.

He said, softly: 'If you're wise, you'll keep quiet.'

A narrowing of the other's eyes was the only response, and Mannering turned again to the contents of the wallet. Several cards read:

MR LAWRENCE WREXFORD
8, COURT MANSIONS
LONDON, W.1.

and two letters were addressed to the same address. Mannering slipped them from their envelopes. They were in different writing, but each started: *'Darling'*.

Mannering tossed them on to the bed.

The return half of a first-class ticket from Waterloo to Winchester, an A.A. membership card, a snapshot of Wrexford in flannels and open-necked shirt, and a hotel bill, comprised the rest of the wallet's contents, apart from some bank and treasury notes. Mannering replaced them, and lifted a suitcase to a table where he could open it while keeping Wrexford in view.

The case was locked, but from Wrexford's pockets he had taken a key-ring. He tried two keys before the case unlocked, and all the time Wrexford's muscles were tense: Mannering could see him straining against the sash-cord.

The lid went back.

Mannering's lips tightened behind his mask, for there was an automatic pistol lying on the top of some discarded linen. He took the gun out, saw that it was fully loaded, and laid it on the table close to his hand.

Mannering explored the case, the interior of which was fully an inch smaller than the outside promised.

That indicated a false bottom.

It was so cunningly concealed that for some seconds he was unable to find it.

Sweat was standing out on Wrexford's forehead. He strained at his bonds, as if he were preparing to make a desperate effort in spite of his tied hands. Mannering picked the gun up.

'Keep quiet, Wrexford. I'll deal with you later.'

The man stiffened, but fell back. Mannering pulled the lid of the false bottom up, and found an envelope beneath it that had once been wax-sealed but was now open. It was then that Wrexford lost his self-control.

He swung his legs wildly, kicking at the table. The effort caused him to overbalance, and he pitched heavily on to the floor. Mannering pulled the man up, pushing him back on to the bed. Wrexford was breathing convulsively, but Mannering knew that he was safe from one thing; for

Wrexford could have attempted to shout, but had not done so.

Wrexford, then was *afraid* to raise an alarm.

The man had exhausted himself, and Mannering backed to the table, taking the papers from the envelope. There were several that seemed ordinary business letters, but a typewritten sheet had a name in one corner which riveted Mannering's attention.

It was:

'*MORENCY*' *August 27th*

Rome:	Tuesday 3rd September. Then	
Berlin:	Wednesday/Thursday, 4th & 5th	Alleno
Bucharest:	Friday/Saturday, 6th & 7th	
Budapest:	Sunday 8th.	
Ankara:	Monday/Tuesday, 9th & 10th	
Athens:	Wednesday 11th	Dimitrios
Zagreb:	Thursday/Friday, 12th & 13th	
Paris:	Saturday/Sunday, 14th & 15th	
Scandin-		Wrexford
avia:	Monday/Tuesday, 16th & 17th	
London:	Wednesday/Tuesday, 18th to 24th	

Mannering lifted his eyes from the paper, and there was cold anger in them. The most important thing that the list told him was that this detailed journey-sheet had been known to someone on August 27th. Before Morency had reached England, someone had been fully aware of his programme, although the Press had not been given that information, and Morency's arrival at the various capitals had been unexpected.

The unknowns Alleno and Dimitrios had been watching him on the Continent, while in France and Scandinavia Wrexford had operated. And now Wrexford's chief object in England was the watching of Morency, even if Logan and Woolf were not aware of it.

Mannering moved over to him and untied the improvised gag, first picking up the automatic.

'Well?' he said.

The man attempted to speak, failed, and tried again. The

sounds that came at last were hoarse and breathless, echoing the fear that showed in his eyes.

'Keep – keep this to yourself! It's worth a fortune!'

Mannering said sharply. 'How much?'

'I'll – I'll pay you a thousand if you'll keep quiet. In cash, I can get it tomorrow. For God's sake don't give me away! It'll mean –'

And then the telephone rang sharply.

It cut across Wrexford's words, and he stopped and stared towards it, his lips set and his eyes wide with alarm. Mannering went rigid, but relaxed as he backed towards the instrument, keeping the gun trained on Wrexford. He lifted the receiver and said 'Who is that?' in a fair imitation of the suave voice Wrexford had used with Logan.

A man's voice, cold and decisive, came clearly.

'Get away at once, Wrexford. Don't ask questions. Leave things as they are and get away.'

'All right.'

'You might have an hour's jump of the police,' the cold voice went on, 'certainly no more. You know where to meet me.'

The line went dead. Mannering turned, alive to the dangers for Wrexford and to himself. He knew that if the police caught the man they would make him talk.

And Wrexford knew Logan's story.

If Wrexford talked, Mannering would take his chance. But he might learn more of the man's activities: there was still time to try.

'A thousand, is it,' he said slowly. 'Think again, and think in big figures.'

'Who – who was that?' gasped Wrexford.

'A friend of yours named Woolf,' Mannering lied easily. 'He's worried about something that happened earlier tonight.' He saw Wrexford's face relax, and then added casually: 'What about those figures, Wrexford? And what guarantee have I got that you'll pay?'

'You damned fool, I've got to pay! I daren't be caught.' Wrexford's lips worked, and his voice took on a deeper, persuasive note. 'It's nothing to you. I – look here, I'll make

79

it two thousand. Two thousand, cash on the nail.'

'You can't give it on the nail,' Mannering said coldly. In his ear the telephone words were echoing: 'You might have an hour's jump of the police'. *Might* was the word that mattered, it meant that the police were on the way and might arrive at any time. He hardened his voice. 'I want a guarantee of some kind. Supposing you tell me where you report with this?' He touched the journey-sheet, watching Wrexford narrowly and seeing the quick suspicion which sprang into the man's eyes.

'That won't help. I –'

He stopped abruptly.

There was a squeal of brakes, followed by the sound of heavy footsteps below.

Silence fell, but lasted only for a moment, the lift gate clanged.

Mannering stepped swiftly to the door. He heard the lift stop, and the mutter of voices. He made sure that the door was locked and bolted, then wedged a chair beneath the handle. A voice said sharply:

'All right, porter, you needn't stay.'

A knock came sharply on the door, but it was the voice which sent alarm sheering through Mannering, a voice he recognised. It belonged to Chief Inspector Bristow, of Scotland Yard, the man he had feared was coming to Vere House.

Mannering felt a quick nausea, but he dared waste no time. He switched off the light, as Bristow's knock came again, hard and authoritative.

Mannering groped his way across the room. He reached the window, and pushed it up. Bristow's voice was raised:

'Open, in the name of the law!'

The dark, cool air rushed about Mannering's forehead. By the faint glow from a car's lights he could see two men.

Bristow's men, of course, there to make sure that no one escaped through the window.

Mannering's mind was cool and alert, conscious of the danger and yet holding without panic to what chance remained.

If he could get back to his room he might get through.

He put one leg over the sill, pushed his head and shoulders through, hearing the banging on the door growing louder and more insistent. He groped with his right hand along the outside wall, touched the framework of a window.

There was a chance!

He pulled himself out, too intent to think of slipping, too desperate to move too slowly. He stood with his feet on the sill of Wrexford's room and his hands gripping the stone-work about the other window, and then he swung outwards putting all his weight on his fingers.

His right hand slipped.

Panic went through him like a white-hot pain, and he grabbed desperately while trying to find the lower sill with his feet. His shoe touched it, but was followed by a beam of light coming upwards from the street and focusing on Wrexford's open window. It moved along, and Mannering saw it about his feet. It betrayed him, but showed him the sill and enabled him to get foothold. Shouts came from the men below.

From farther away there was a crash: Bristow had forced the door of Wrexford's room.

Mannering swayed backwards, unable to escape the beam of light shining on his back. With his free hand he pulled at the window. It opened abruptly, and as he swung himself through he caught a glimpse of a red-faced man in pyjamas.

Mannering reached the door, took the key out, slipped through to the empty but lighted passage, then locked the door behind him.

Then, for the first time, he hesitated. If he passed Wrexford's room, Bristow might see him. He glanced in the other direction. Relief surged through him when he saw a narrow flight of stairs.

Before he reached them a yell came from the room he had passed through, and a frantic hammering. A voice was raised:

'*Next door – fast!*'

Mannering reached the second floor, finding a passage

81

similar to that below. He stepped towards Room 9 and entered it as a door in the passage opened, and a nervous voice called:

'*Here – what's up?*'

The shouting and banging continued from below, but was deadened as Mannering closed the door. He was breathing hard, but he dared not relax. A search of the hotel was inevitable, and he had to get away; he dared not come face to face with Bristow.

He glanced round swiftly to make sure he had left nothing, then switched off the light and, cautiously, pushed the window up. He heard no sound of movement and saw nothing, but there was sure to be one of Bristow's men guarding the back. He waited, accustoming his eyes to the darkness, and then estimating the drop.

It was twenty feet or more: he dared not risk a jump.

He was working swiftly, reckoning only on the chances of a getaway, forgetful of all other issues. His mind had slipped automatically back to the days of the Baron, and it was the Baron who ripped the clothes from the bed, tied two sheets together, and then, fastening one end of them to the foot of the bed, wound the other about his arm, and climbed through the window. The sheet pulled taut as he went down. He could not see the ground, but when the sheets had run their full length he lowered his legs cautiously.

He dropped.

For a sickening second he thought that the gap would prove to be too great. Then his feet touched the ground with a jarring impact. He staggered forward.

And then the beam of a torch shone straight into his face.

He stood motionless, his eyes narrowed, his fists clenched. A man said with satisfaction.

'Oh no, you don't!'

Mannering went forward.

He could see only the white orb of the torch, and nothing of the man behind it, but he dashed the torch away and then struck out. His fist caught the other in the stomach, and the man lurched forward, staggered, and fell.

Vaguely Mannering could see the roof of the next building.

Was the courtyard of the White Angel walled?

It was not.

Mannering reached a cobbled drive-in, dived through an open gate, and found himself in the High Street. Then he heard Bristow's voice:

'Get round to the back both of you!'

Mannering stepped, a little unsteadily, into the road, wrenching off his scarf and slipping it into his pocket. The dim lights from several parked cars guided him to the M.G.

Thankfully, he slipped into the driving-seat.

*　　*　　*

Some time after Mannering had driven away, Chief Inspector William Bristow sat in the Superintendent's office at the Winchester police station, and spoke into the telephone.

'Yes, sir,' he said. 'I've got Wrexford, with all the papers we need to prove the case against him. There's no evidence who he was working for, though.'

'That will come. Anything else?'

'There was someone else with him before us. Wrexford swears he does not know who.'

'Have you any idea?' The voice of Sir David Ffoulkes, Assistant Commissioner of Scotland Yard, sharpened.

'No sir,' said Bristow. 'It was someone after Wrexford, that's all we do know. There is another thing, though. As we thought, Wrexford was working under cover of the Woolf Agency. He was retaining them at a good fee, but Woolf says that he was employed only to watch Lady Usk's jewels. I doubt whether Woolf or the man Logan know what Wrexford's real game was.'

'You want to leave them, is that it?'

'I think it would be wise, sir,' said Bristow cautiously. 'I can have them watched and if they do know more than I think, we'll find out better by giving them enough rope. Is that in order?'

'I'll leave it to you, Bristow. Wrexford's the man we were anxious about. Your principal down there should be pleased.'

Bristow's lips relaxed in a smile.

'I hope so, sir. I'll go along and see him in the morning, and see what this burglary looks like, too. But I doubt if it's connected with the visitor. If it was, Wrexford was behind it, and we'll soon have the facts.'

'All right,' said the A.C. slowly. 'Handle it with the utmost discretion, Bristow.'

'I'll watch everything, sir,' said Bristow with confidence.

There was a slight pause, and then the Assistant Commissioner said casually:

'I'm sure you will. Including Mannering, Bristow.'

'*Who?*'

The bellow brought no more than a dry chuckle from the Assistant Commissioner.

'Why, yes, I've just been informed that he's down there. I believe Mr Vere is consulting him about the robbery.'

Slowly Bristow replaced the receiver, and stared grimly across the office.

'So the Baron's down there, is he? Now I wonder – '

He was thinking of the report that a plainclothes man at the back of the house had given, and a statement from the red-faced man through whose room the unknown had escaped. Both had testified to a scarf tied across the lower half of the unknown man's face.

Was it coincidence that the Baron had so often used a scarf in just such a way?

Bristow pulled the telephone towards him, and calling Martin Vere, said that he would be there by midnight.

CHAPTER 11

Bristow's Questions

The likely thing for Bristow to do, reasoned Mannering, was to visit Vere House as soon as Wrexford was in the police cell. If Bristow reached the house that night it would not necessarily mean that he had any reason for associating the Baron with the night's escapade. But Mannering felt on edge, aware of the impossibility of hiding the fact that he had been out. Probably Vere would volunteer a statement to that effect; evasion was out of the question, and he had to find a reasonable explanation, or at least one which Bristow would be unable to disprove.

He had thrown the automatic and the necklace into some bushes in a narrow lane. At least they would not be found easily.

The drive gates were open, and he reached the garage as a clock struck eleven. He put the M.G. away, locked the garage door and put the key over the lintel. When he reached the hall Ransome was leaving the drawing-room. The butler turned towards him, not trying to hide his curiosity.

'How long has Logan been back?' Mannering put disappointment into his voice and his expression.

'Well over half-an-hour, sir.'

'I lost him,' said Mannering disgustedly. 'Where's Mr Vere?'

'I think everyone who has not gone to bed, sir, is in here.' Ransome opened the drawing-room door, and Mannering went through. The Veres, Lorna, Menzies and Dryden – the poet talking earnestly to Hilda Markham, the economist – were there. Dryden looked up sharply.

None of the others showed any particular interest, but it was not long before Hilda Markham declared it was time she went to bed. Menzies and Dryden rose with her, and as the Veres saw all three of their guests to the foot of the stairs, Lorna turned quickly to Mannering.

'What went wrong?' she said quietly.

'Bristow's in Winchester.'

'Did you see him?'

'I heard him,' Mannering said, 'but we didn't meet face to face. My story for the Veres is that I confused the Daimler with another, and I've spent the past hour or so on a wild goose chase. I'll slip into your room later with details. Were you able to check up on Cecilie?'

'She went to bed all right,' Lorna said.

As she spoke, the Veres rejoined them.

Vere was plainly disappointed by the story, but it was Diana's reaction which Mannering studied more closely. Though she hid her disappointment at the failure of the chase, there was no disguising her apprehension.

Vere said at last:

'Oh, well, it can't be helped. A good night's rest won't do us any harm.' He yawned, and at that moment the telephone rang.

Vere lifted the receiver, listened, and then spoke in surprise: 'Tonight? Well, of course, Inspector. I'd no idea you were coming so soon, but I'll be glad to see you . . . goodbye.' He turned to the others, his eyes lively again. 'You were right, Mannering – it's an Inspector named Bristow. He's in Winchester now, and he's coming straight out. So we won't be able to get to bed just yet.'

'He's lost no time,' said Diana.

Mannering fancied that she wished he had; if so, he heartily agreed with her. It was useless to tell himself that it was unlikely Bristow had reason to suspect his presence at the White Angel. He was anxious, even apprehensive. The porter had not seen enough of him for identification, but the red-faced man in the bedroom might have done so.

'If you'll forgive me, I think I'll get along,' he said. 'If Bristow wants me, I'll be awake.'

There was a chorus of goodnights and Mannering and Lorna went out. She said urgently:

'Is there much risk?'

'Practically none,' Mannering answered, but the words lacked conviction. Once in his room, he related the essentials of the encounter briefly, and then went on: 'Wrexford's a spy watching Morency, and the police found evidence to arrest him. As Bristow was coming out this way he was the obvious man for the job. It's as straight-forward as that.'

'Is it?' asked Lorna. 'Apart from the possibility that you could be recognised, there's the call Wrexford made to Woolf.'

'Why should Wrexford talk about it?' asked Mannering.

'That depends whether there's any reason for Bristow to think of you,' Lorna insisted. 'If there is, he'll question Wrexford more closely, and Logan's story might come out. Logan *will* talk sooner or later, he's not the type who can keep quiet.'

Mannering forced a smile. 'Aren't you a bit pessimistic? After all, he earns his living as an inquiry agent.'

'John' – her voice was low – 'I don't want to make things look worse than they are, but you've got to be alive to the possibilities.'

Mannering said bitterly: 'I'm alive to them all right, but there's just nothing more I can do. After all,' he added, 'I didn't rob the lady. Although it looks as if the quicker I find out who did the better. I'm going to get into a dressing-gown,' he added more briskly. 'If Bristow comes that might encourage him to think that I wasn't expecting him.'

When she had gone, Mannering prepared leisurely for bed. By midnight, no visitor having arrived, he decided that he was to be left in peace.

But it was an hour before he went to sleep.

Bristow, meanwhile, having heard Vere's story and learned that Mannering had been out, had decided that a night of uncertainty might worry Mannering far more than an immediate call.

'Always assuming,' Bristow admitted to himself, 'that

Mannering was there tonight. Whoever it was, certainly left me Wrexford on a plate. That's a point to consider.'

*   *   *

Mannering awakened to find the sun shining. In spite of this, he was filled with a sense of disquiet which he did not immediately place.

His wristwatch showed him that it was twenty-past eight. Tea would be brought up in ten minutes. He put his hands behind his head, eased himself up on the pillows, and started to think.

Then he realised what had caused his misgivings.

Lady Usk, Cecilie, the men in the grounds, Tommy's misfortune, Morency's quiet acceptance of a disturbance which could so easily upset his plans, Dryden's oddness – all those items faded into insignificance against the journey to Winchester, and the finding of the paste gems in his drawer.

Who had put them there?

He recalled Lady Usk's manner, and then remembered that her husband was due that morning. Usk was poor in his own right, and depended largely on his wife for his income. Cecilie also was dependent on her stepmother. But were either motives strong enough to inspire theft?

Cecilie, Deverell, Usk himself – and even Tommy Armitage – might feel homicidal towards Lady Usk, but while she remained alive there was no legal reason why they should not. At the moment she seemed more the villain of the piece than the victim, although Mannering wondered whether he was doing her an injustice.

Certainly he did not feel as well-disposed towards her as he had on the previous night.

He finished his tea, bathed and dressed, puzzled by Bristow's non-appearance, but feeling more cheerful. Glancing out of the window, he saw Cecilie and Lorna walking across the lawns. Lorna, then, had been down early, and had lost no time in making friends with Cecilie. It was like her to concentrate on that: both of them realised the importance of solving the problem.

He went downstairs.

Lorna and Cecilie were coming into the breakfast room through french windows as he entered.

'Are the others late or early?' he asked.

'Late,' said the economist. She looked younger than Mannering had imagined, and behind her horn-rimmed glasses her blue eyes were shrewd and alert. She spoke crisply:

'Well, Mr Mannering, are you studying our likely crime repressions?'

'Certainly not at breakfast,' said Mannering laughing.

Miss Markham gave an exaggerated sigh. 'You're as flippant as everyone else. What's happened to Tommy? He's usually among the first down.'

Mannering helped himself to Kedgeree.

'I don't know,' he said. 'Wasn't he out walking last night?'

'He disappeared in the middle of a rubber, and as a result I lost four and ninepence,' said Miss Markham with some asperity.

Mannering smiled. 'You should study the economic aspect of gambling, Miss Markham. Once you start you'll either give up gambling or economics.'

'Let us change the subject,' said Hilda Markham, with mock acerbity. 'How is your step-mother, Cecilie?'

'She's staying in bed until lunch-time,' said Cecilie. Mannering noted that she had lost all trace of the agitation which she had shown on the previous evening, and it occurred to him that in his review of the night's events he had forgotten the meeting with Cecilie, and the cry he had imagined she had uttered. Now he recalled that she had lied – for she had told him she had stumbled on the rose walk, and he knew she had been on the other side of the garden. Yet it was hard to believe that Cecilie would lie without a strong reason. She looked young, fresh and vivid, as if she had been relieved of a considerable burden. Could that be due altogether to the fact that she was having a morning's freedom from her step-mother?

Dryden came down ten minutes later, preoccupied and

barely acknowledging the others' presence. He was followed by Menzies, a youngster of twenty-one or two. Menzies was in uniform, with a lieutenant's two stars on his shoulder.

'What a life,' he said, stepping briskly to the hot plate. 'Camp and training again after today. Has anyone left anything?' He helped himself liberally. 'Where's Tommy?'

'Everyone wants to know where Tommy is,' said Hilda Markham.

'Everyone can know,' said Diana Vere as she entered. 'He went for a walk last night, his torch failed, and he had a nasty tumble.'

'Oh-ho!' said Menzies. 'I wonder who lured him out? It wouldn't be you, would it, Cecilie?'

'Eat your breakfast,' said Hilda sharply. 'What a pity children learn to speak before they're twenty-one.'

But Menzies was irrepressible. 'Where's your celebrity, Di?' he went on happily, 'or is he yet another blackout casualty? What time did he arrive last night, by the way?'

'Late,' said Diana calmly. 'And if you talk much more you'll lose your train.'

But there was still no sign of Bristow.

It was Lorna who suggested a walk after breakfast. Dryden hesitated, and then announced solemnly that he was in the middle of a composition.

Cecilie, Miss Markham, Mannering and Lorna elected to walk.

'I take it,' said Lorna as she went upstairs for a headscarf, 'that you want to talk to Cecilie?'

Mannering nodded.

'What's Bristow doing?'

'Nothing about me, my sweet. We were too gloomy last night.'

Lorna smiled, but she was not convinced. She covered her feelings well, however, and for twenty minutes the four walked in line. Then Lorna called Hilda Markham away to admire a view, and Mannering went ahead with Cecilie. She looked at him soberly as he said:

'How is the patient?'

'She's much too quiet. It seems to have affected her more

than I thought it would. Her heart isn't too good, I know.'

'She'll get over it,' said Mannering easily. 'Can you bear it if I ask you one or two questions that may seem odd?'

'I'll try.'

'Thanks. First of all, how long has she had the Deverell necklace?'

'Oh – about a month.'

'And how long have you thought she seemed frightened?' Cecilie looked straight ahead of her.

'About the same time I suppose.'

'Then there's another thing. Lady Usk seemed to be prejudiced against jewel-merchants – do you know why?'

'That's an easy one,' said Cecilie. 'She found she could buy cheaper by going direct to – to the seller. She got the Deverell necklace for ten thous – ' Cecilie stopped, and then went on awkwardly: 'I suppose it's hardly fair to talk about that, but you know what I was going to say.'

'But I'll assume you didn't say it,' said Mannering. 'Now here's something that will startle you. Did you ever know her to have replicas made of her jewels?'

Cecilie turned her face away abruptly, but Mannering saw that she had coloured. He was startled, but made no sign that he had noticed her confusion. She recovered herself well. 'No, I didn't know of any replicas. Are there any?'

'I'm not sure,' lied Mannering. He felt suddenly that it was unwise to trust Cecilie too far: her confusion and her mysterious jaunt on the previous evening perturbed him. How sincere *were* her answers?

He was not sorry when Hilda Markham decided that they had walked far enough, and called them back. There was no further opportunity for talking with Cecilie, but once or twice he caught her looking at him, and in her eyes there was an expression that could have been fear.

It was a little past twelve when they reached the house, and one of the first things Mannering saw was a black-and-green Morris 12 standing outside the garage. He recognised the car as Bristow's. The sight of it brought the personal issue more sharply to his mind, and with it a return of the apprehension of the previous night.

Lorna walked upstairs with him.

'You saw the car?'

Mannering nodded. He closed his door behind them, and leaned with his back against it. 'There was one thing in favour of those bad old days, sweetheart. We did know where we stood, and if the police were after me I had asked for it.'

'That doesn't make the present situation any better. Did you get anything from Cecilie?'

'Enough to make me wonder.'

There was a sharp tap on the door. Mannering opened it, surprised at the quick beating of his heart. But there was nothing in his expression to suggest what he was feeling, and he contrived to mingle pleasure with surprise when he saw who was there.

'Why, Bill Bristow!'

'Hallo, Mannering,' said Chief Inspector Bristow quietly. 'May I come in?'

'Of course. And you two don't need introducing, do you?' Mannering looked at Lorna.

Bristow smiled, and it was not unattractive. He was a good-looking man if in no way distinguished. About him there was a crisp, military air, and his lined but fresh-complexioned face, his greying hair, had not altered from when Mannering had last seen him. He nodded to Lorna affably.

'Good morning, Miss Fauntley.' He turned back to Mannering.

'We needn't beat about the bush, need we? I've had Anderson's report.' He smiled a little but his eyes were hard. 'It seems that you were in the dressing room before anyone else. What took you there?'

Mannering said easily: 'Apparently you haven't talked with Mr Vere.'

'Just what does that mean?' asked Bristow sharply.

'He would hardly have forgotten to tell you that he asked me to come down because of earlier trouble,' Mannering said, and he smiled lazily. 'Everyone doesn't harbour the same ill-will as you, Bill. If you can forget your notion about the Baron, you'll remember that I have been known to chase crooks. Vere knew about that, and acted on it.'

'There are some things he didn't know,' Bristow said, 'or you wouldn't have been here. Are you claiming that you went to the dressing-room because you were working on the – er – case?'

'I'm not claiming – I'm telling you.'

Bristow said nothing, and Mannering went on:

'Bristow, I've a fair idea of your difficulties here. With Morency on the spot you want to keep this business quiet, even from the staff. Officially I suppose you're here because of Morency, but with his papers on the premises you don't want light fingers close at hand. I could help, you know.'

'Oh, could you.'

Mannering felt a sharp irritation.

'I have in the past. Why not again?'

Bristow fingered his chin.

'You seem to forget, Mannering, that there's been a big jewel robbery. It's odd that you're so often on the spot, too odd for me to take chances. Mr Vere may have invited you to investigate, but your efforts to prevent the theft weren't successful. I've taken over, and I don't want interference.'

Mannering forced back a sharp answer, knowing that when he chose to be Bristow was immovable, understanding the other's motives and yet wondering whether the rejections of his offer would have been so final had there been no suspicion of activity on the previous night. Bristow had given no hint, yet his manner suggested a sharp hostility.

'All right,' Mannering said. 'We understand each other. I don't want to disturb your arrangements,' he added sarcastically, 'but you have been known to go wrong, when I've been right. If it looks like happening again I'll try to prove it.'

Bristow was suave. 'I can't force you into any position, Mannering – yet.'

'And you won't,' said Mannering with spirit. 'Didn't you learn that I urged Vere to send for the police when I first heard of the theft?'

'I suppose that's something.' Bristow had relaxed, and

93

was taking a cigarette from his case.

'It's true,' said Mannering. 'I advised the police because (a) I had no desire to be involved in serious investigations, (b) because I knew that if the local police turned it over to the Yard you would immediately rake up your old suspicions, and (c) because I wanted the thing cleared up quickly. Have you any complaints?'

'No.' Bristow sounded thoughtful.

'That's fine,' said Mannering warmly. 'Now if you think it's necessary to go into the movements of the guests, I'll tell you what I can. Or if you prefer to work on your own, that suits me. But you can take it as certain,' went on Mannering, 'that I won't take kindly to being singled out as the most likely suspect. Try to rid your mind of hoary fancies – for instance, that I'm the Baron – and start from scratch.'

'Hm-hm,' said Bristow. He blew smoke towards the ceiling, and his grey eyes smiled at Lorna. 'What happened in the grounds when you found Mr Armitage, unconscious?'

Mannering smiled ruefully.

'I didn't get far, Bill. It wasn't my night out. I saw a little fellow I didn't recognise, and went after him. He stopped me with a brick.'

'Oh, I remember Mr Vere mentioning that,' said Bristow with transparent ingenuousness. 'No ill effects I hope?'

'Nothing to worry about.'

'Good! Now, I'm as anxious to get to the bottom of this as you appear to be. I can say to you what I can't say to the others. Since Mr Vere's taken you into his confidence in some measure, you know the importance of Mr Morency's visit. There will be other politicians here over the weekend, and it's important that there should be no trouble – as you said,' he added quickly. 'Obviously with a suspected thief in the house, documents can't be considered safe. The thief must be found, or' – Bristow shrugged – 'Mr Vere will be asked to arrange for all his guests to leave, for the time being. They will be watched, of course, in view of the suspicions aroused, but they won't be here.'

Mannering surveyed the Inspector through narrowed eyes.

94

'That seems a bit drastic,' he said. 'If you'd said so before I could have understood why you turned down my offer, Bill.'

'Could you?' asked Bristow. He tapped the ash off his cigarette, and his voice sharpened. 'Mannering, what did you visit Wrexford for? What did you take from his room?'

Chapter 12

Bristow Attacks

A pulse throbbed in Mannering's forehead, but otherwise he showed no sign of strain. As he met Bristow's cold and accusing eyes he was thinking quickly.

Bristow had some grounds for the scarcely veiled accusation or he would not have made it. But had he any kind of proof he would have acted differently. Bristow, then, needed to substantiate his suspicions.

Mannering said slowly: 'That has all the marks of a catch question, Bristow. I don't like your manner.'

'Never mind what you like,' Bristow snapped. 'What do you know about Wrexford?'

The worst moment had passed; Bristow had hoped to break down Mannering's confidence, but he had failed.

'It would be a help if I knew who you meant, and what you meant,' Mannering said coldly.

'Oh, would it?' said Bristow grimly. 'All right, I'll tell you. You followed Logan into Winchester last night and learned that he visited Wrexford. You broke in on the man later and took something from his room. You were seen, Mannering.'

'Seen, was I?' Mannering had relaxed, and there was mockery in his smile; inwardly he was far from confident. 'It would be interesting to know the man with the magic eyes, Bristow. I went in the Basingstoke direction, and I wasn't pleased at wasting my time.'

'That might suit Vere, but it doesn't satisfy me.'

'You're always so difficult to satisfy,' said Mannering gently. 'Let's have the man or men who saw me up here.

They'll find their mistake, and it might persuade you to cool down.'

Bristow said sharply. 'Mannering, I'd like a word with you in my room.'

Mannering shrugged, but the tension had returned. Bristow had not yet revealed his hand, and was playing a cool, deliberate game. Mannering decided that it would be better to do what Bristow asked than to protest and show nervousness, wiser to find just what Bristow could do. He had some information – and if it concerned Logan's story it might prove damning.

Yet Bristow had not acted as if he had any reason for suspecting Mannering in the Usk robbery.

That meant nothing; Bristow suspected the Baron had been at Winchester and was playing on that angle; but he could switch over swiftly, might yet pull a bluff against which Mannering had little defence. The uncertainty was nerve-racking; it was better to know the worst.

'All right,' Mannering said.

He opened the door and they both went out, conscious of Lorna's intense gaze behind them. Bristow's lips were set, and he gave an impression of confidence; but that also might be bluff.

Mannering's expression held a faint amusement as he followed the Inspector. Bristow stopped at a door, hesitated and then opened it an inch or two.

'Will you go first?' he said.

Mannering felt his heart racing. Bristow had set a trap, he was putting to the test something which might yet break down the uncertain alibi. With an effort Mannering kept his face expressionless.

He went in.

He felt a spasm of alarm and fear – for a second was afraid that he had given himself away. Then he rallied, as he eyed the two men within. He recognised them at once.

Bristow had brought the White Angel's porter and the burly, red-faced man whom Mannering had threatened with the gun.

Mannering looked at Bristow and spoke sharply, his voice very different from the one the porter had heard.

'There's less privacy here than downstairs, Bristow!'

He was afraid that his bluff would fail, afraid that one man or the other would claim recognition.

Bristow spoke in mock surprise: 'Dear me, I'd forgotten these gentlemen! Would you mind waiting for five minutes?' He smiled at the two men. They had been primed to expect the request, of course, after making their quick inspection.

Mannering's mind worked fast. If they went outside and Bristow questioned them later, he would have no idea of the result of the identification test. It was time to force Bristow's hand, time to turn to the attack. He said abruptly:

'A moment, please. Bristow, I want an explanation of this. You knew these men were here – why did you bring me up?'

'Now, Mr Mannering – ' Bristow was suave.

'I've had more than enough from you this morning,' Mannering snapped. 'Innuendo can go too far, Inspector. You may think I'm investigating this business on my own, you may even want to prove it, but I object to a police trap of this nature.' He swung round on the porter.

'Have either of you seen me before?'

It was a tense moment, one in which his bluff might collapse. The porter would be easy to handle, but the red-faced man might be difficult. Mannering eyed him narrowly, while the porter said nervously:

'Why, no, sir – I don't know you.'

The red-faced man turned to Bristow.

'This isn't the man I saw, Inspector. Now I must get away, I haven't all day to waste.'

Mannering felt a profound relief. He took out a cigarette and lit it slowly, his eyes challenging Bristow's. Bristow's lips tightened; his chagrin at the way the interview had turned in Mannering's favour was plain. But he recovered himself well.

'All right, Mr Benson, thank you. You can go too, Simms.' He opened the door, and the two men went out – Benson without turning, the porter with a nervous glance over his shoulder.

Bristow said thinly. 'Your luck will break one day, Mannering.'

'Luck?' said Mannering. 'Come, Bill, you ought to know that truth will out. Still, I'm beginning to see your angle. You've a case against this fellow Wrexford, have you? Logan probably did the inside work and Wrexford, whoever he is, finished it off. But the jewels weren't with your man – is that it?'

'If there's anything more I want you for, I'll tell you,' Bristow said coldly. 'I won't need you for the time being.'

'This isn't like you,' Mannering said judiciously. 'What's got under your skin?'

'I'm damned if – ' Bristow began harshly. Then he stopped, and Mannering saw the change in his expression, felt his own confidence justified, for Bristow would never have changed so abruptly had he any knowledge of Logan's story. In Bristow there had always been a saving sense of humour, even when things were going badly for him; and now he laughed with genuine amusement. 'Oh, all right, Mannering. I've a call to make, and then I'll come down and see you again. There are one or two things you might help me with.'

Mannering chuckled. 'At your service, as always – and more useful,' he added, 'when not under suspicion.'

He went out and walked briskly to his room. Lorna was standing by the window. She turned quickly.

'It's all right?'

'For the time being,' Mannering said, and told her briefly what had happened. Then: 'He's getting cunning, is Bill Bristow. We'll have to watch him. He's no less dangerous when he's affable, and he'll have a lot to think about when he does get Logan's story. I wonder what he's doing about Logan?' Mannering added. 'It wouldn't surprise me if he doesn't give the man plenty of rope to hang himself.'

'Or you,' said Lorna drily.

Bristow was back within ten minutes, and at Mannering's invitation sat down on the edge of the bed. There was no sign of his earlier abruptness: the accusation might never have been made.

99

'Well, now, Mannering, we were talking about the trouble here. You're right, of course, about the importance of taking no risks with Mr Morency at the house. Suspicion is sufficient for detention on some counts, without a warrant.' There was a bark in the last sentence, but Mannering ignored it.

'Some counts meaning espionage?'

'Could be,' Bristow said airily. 'I want to clear everything up without embarrassing Mrs Vere if I can, and I'm checking the movements of the guests.'

'Why not start on the servants?'

'They're clear. If you're thinking of Logan's trip last night you'll like to know that there's no known connection between that and the theft except as far as Logan's work for Lady Usk is concerned. Now – ' His manner grew more decisive. 'You've an hour to account for – between eight forty-five when the jewels were put into the safe, and nine forty-five when it was discovered they were missing. It shouldn't be hard.'

'It isn't,' Mannering said. He distrusted Bristow's apparent frankness, but answered easily: 'The party broke up about nine-fifteen. I went into the garden soon afterwards.'

'Why?' Bristow asked.

'I wanted to see Miss Grey,' Mannering admitted. 'I followed her along the rose-walk, but lost her. Then I saw Morency arrive. Miss Grey returned within a few minutes, and I talked with her outside the drawing-room door. We entered the room together, and she went upstairs. I followed practically on her heels, and heard Lady Usk call out. Armitage was at the card-room door and heard the cry at the same time.' Mannering met Bristow's eyes squarely. 'That's all I can tell you.'

Bristow fingered his moustache.

'There was just time for you to get upstairs, but hardly enough for you to open the safe and get away before Lady Usk reached her room. After all, you're out of practice – I think! – and you can't work miracles with a safe of that type.'

'I was never *in* practice,' said Mannering sharply.

'Well, well,' said Bristow comfortably, 'let's leave it at that. Your story agrees with the others, and personally I'm glad.' Ignoring his earlier attitude, he went on confidentially: 'Between you and me, I'm a little doubtful of Lady Usk's story. Her daughter says that she keeps the purse with her always, and has never been known to leave it behind. It was odd that she left it yesterday afternoon – or don't you think so?'

'It could look odd,' Mannering said.

'Yes. You'd hardly miss that point. One of the puzzling angles of the case so far is that Lady Usk has been so anxious to talk to you.' Bristow's voice was bland. 'You're not a particular friend of hers, are you?'

'No,' said Mannering. 'She wanted me to see her jewels, and I honoured her.'

'Hmm,' said Bristow. 'What did she say to you when you talked with her alone? Miss Grey says you were in the room for nearly twenty minutes.'

Again the atmosphere had grown tense, and Mannering knew that Bristow had seen the possibility that the peeress had not told the truth. Clearly Bristow doubted whether the robbery was what it appeared to be on the surface.

Mannering could remember his talk with Lady Usk vividly. Her fear, her excitement, reaching at one time to a point of hysteria, and her insistence that he should say nothing to the police. It was plain that Bristow was satisfied the Baron had not opened the safe, but still he believed Mannering might know more than he admitted. To get at the truth, Bristow had taken a high-hand, and then, with a fine show of confidence, suggested that since Mannering was quite clear of suspicion, there was no object in hiding facts.

Mannering said: 'I was with her twenty minutes or so. I had the impression that she was frightened, and she told me she employed a detective to watch her. But I think there's a very simple explanation of her wanting to see me.'

'Yes?' Bristow was eager.

'She was conscious of being disliked,' said Mannering, 'and she believed I would be more sympathetic than the others. It's a reasonable enough attitude, Bill.'

'Oh,' said Bristow disappointedly. 'There's nothing else?
What do you mean by "she was frightened"?'

'I didn't even say it,' said Mannering. 'I said I had that
impression, but it might have been the result of the shock of
finding the safe open. She fainted right out, you know. I'm
told her heart's not too steady.'

'You didn't mean more than that?' Bristow insisted.

'I didn't,' said Mannering firmly.

'Hmm. Did you see that little purse of hers, Mannering?'

'Yes.'

'She had it tucked inside her dress, didn't she?'

'Yes.' A little pulse was tickling at Mannering's forehead,
for he was acutely conscious of the moment when the purse
had been opened, and the pencilled threat had been handed
to him. Had Bristow any inkling of that oddly-worded
missive? Was Bristow still playing a cat-and-mouse game
with the deliberate intention of trying to trick him?

'There was nothing in it besides the combination code?'
Bristow went on.

'I don't know what else,' said Mannering, wishing Lady
Usk had not sworn him to silence.

'Hmm.' Bristow frowned. 'She showed me the purse, but
she wouldn't let me look into it. It's a peculiar affair altogether. Was Miss Grey in the drawing-room all the time
before she went out, do you know?'

'No,' said Mannering. 'She wasn't there for more than
two or three minutes. I think she went upstairs to get a coat.'

'That's what she told me,' said Bristow. He shrugged.
'Well, it's awkward. The servants are quite clear – thanks
to a Variety broadcast we know that.'

Mannering said slowly: 'It narrows things down pretty
well. Either someone came in from the outside, or it was one
of the guests. What about this Wrexford fellow?'

'Forget him,' said Bristow. 'I don't mind telling you,
Mannering, that the only guests not accounted for – apart
from your few minutes in the garden' – he broke off with a
sly smile – 'are Miss Grey, Lady Usk, Mr Armitage, and
that rather sharp-faced woman – what's her name?'

Mannering felt surprised.

'You mean Miss Markham?'

'Yes, that's her. Ruling you out, and assuming that Lady Usk wouldn't rob herself, it narrows down to three people. They were all upstairs and in their rooms – they say – for at least twenty minutes of the hour we're worried about.' Bristow fingered his moustache thoughtfully, and then went on: 'Do you know Mr Armitage well?'

'No,' said Mannering. 'I've known him slightly for years, though, and if you think Tommy Armitage is your man, I'd say you were wrong. Why rule out the possibility that someone came from the outside?'

Bristow smiled. 'Whoever opened the safe knew the combination, and the combination had to be taken from Lady Usk's purse during the afternoon.'

'A servant could have learned the combination and telephoned it to someone outside,' said Mannering drily.

'I see you're still labouring the Logan point.'

'Logan apart,' said Mannering, 'you seem to be ignoring the men Armitage saw in the grounds. He's quite sure of himself, you know, and I chased one man myself.'

Bristow shrugged. 'Yes, I know. But Morency might have been followed, and if he was being watched the watchers would not want to be seen.' The words were casual enough, yet Mannering knew Bristow had Wrexford in mind. But Wrexford had claimed no knowledge of the visit to the grounds, and had been anxious to learn more about it. Did Bristow know that? He wished he could learn how much Wrexford had said.

'Why should Mr Morency be watched?' asked Lorna ingenuously.

'Well,' said Bristow, 'he's a gentleman of some importance, you know. A lot of people would like to know why he's here, and what he's doing. Which doesn't affect the job I'm on,' added Bristow. 'Mannering – you'll be frank, I hope. Do you know of anything that might help me?'

'No,' said Mannering. 'I don't know of anything about the robbery itself that could give you a scrap of help.'

'You've qualified that pretty stringently,' said Bristow.

'That's the main subject you're interested in, isn't it?' said Mannering blandly. 'How long are you staying, Bill?'

'Until Morency goes back,' said Bristow, relaxing and clasping his hands about one knee. 'Hallo, what's that?'

Mannering smiled. 'A knock on the door, Bill.' He stepped across the room, opened the door, and saw Diana. She was breathing hard, and her eyes were sparkling angrily.

'I want to see the Inspector,' she said quickly. 'Mr Bristow, will you please come along to Mr Armitage's room.'

Bristow was on his feet at once.

'Of course. What's happened?'

'He went out for a walk twenty minutes ago,' said Diana tensely, 'and when he reached his room again his safe had been opened. There isn't much missing, but there's enough. You'd better come too, John.'

CHAPTER 13

More of Lady Usk

Bristow and Mannering reached Armitage's room only a step or two behind Diana.

Armitage was standing in front of an open safe with an expression of startled surprise. It was possible to believe that he had stood there staring uncomprehendingly from the moment he had told Diana what had happened.

Bristow dropped to his knees beside the safe.

'How much was in it, sir?'

'Oh, about thirty pounds in cash. And some oddments, you know. Studs and cuff-links, worth fifty or sixty, I suppose. Family stuff, you know.'

'I suppose you left the safe locked?'

Tommy looked a little shamefaced. 'Well, yes. But the numbers were written down on a scrap of paper, and I left it on the dressing-table.' He pointed to a piece of notepaper held down by a hairbrush. 'A bit careless, I suppose.'

'A *bit* careless,' said Bristow heavily. 'Yes, I think we can say that, Mr Armitage. I'd like my man up, Mrs Vere.'

Diana nodded towards the house telephone, and Bristow lifted the receiver and rang through for Detective Sergeant Tring. That done, he turned to the others, and said pleasantly. 'I won't keep you any longer for the present.'

Quietly they left the room and made their way to Martin Vere's study. Diana sat down heavily in the largest chair, which completely engulfed her.

'What Vicky will say I don't know,' she said wearily. 'And we've two guests from Whitehall due this afternoon.' Her expression was one of utter defeat, but Mannering knew she would soon regain her spirits. 'What the devil *are* we going to do?'

Armitage looked ill-at-ease.

'Well, you can blame me, if it'll do you any good. It wouldn't have happened if I hadn't been such a fool as to leave that paper about.'

'Don't be an ass,' said Diana comfortingly. 'The thief would have been here, even if there had been nothing to take.' She eyed Mannering hopefully. 'John, what did the Inspector say to you? Has he any idea who took the jewels last night?'

'No,' said Mannering. 'Or if he had he didn't tell me.'

'I suppose this was done by the same cove,' said Tommy tentatively.

'Were the notes big ones?'

'There were one or two fives, yes.'

'Did you have the numbers?'

'Numbers?' said Tommy. 'No, I didn't. But I daresay the Bank would know. If – ' He stopped and rubbed his chin. 'If I got 'em from a bank, that is. I changed a twenty at a night club before I came down.'

Diana shrugged resignedly. 'Well, there's nothing we can do about it. If you're going out, John, you might go towards the village. Martin and Vicky have gone for a walk in that direction, and they'd better know as soon as possible.'

'I'll go at once,' Mannering promised.

As he walked across the landing he heard Lorna's voice coming from Cecilie's room.

He smiled with satisfaction. Lorna had understood, from that nod, what he had wanted her to do. Clearly Cecilie was the most likely suspect from the point of view of the jewel-robbery, and there were several things the girl had done which were not explained. Her lies of the previous night when she had claimed to be in the rose-garden, and her perturbation at mention of paste jewels were points in Mannering's mind. There was, too, the cry, as of alarm.

Had she met one or more of the men known to have been prowling about the grounds?

He disliked the thought, but had to consider it. It was

essential to find the thief – and find him or her before Bristow heard Logan's story. He felt uneasy: why was Bristow so quiet and inactive about Logan?

He pushed his disquiet aside.

With luck Lorna would find out whether Cecilie had been in a position to enter Armitage's room. If the girl was unable to prove she had been elsewhere, it would look very black against her.

If the two robberies had been committed by the same person, Armitage was in the clear, although there was as much reason to believe Armitage would rob his own room as that Lady Usk would steal her own jewels. Barring, of course, the possibility that Tommy had staged the second burglary to clear himself of suspicion of the first.

Assuming that there *had* been two genuine robberies, only Cecilie and Hilda Markham were on the list of suspects among the guests. Mannering knew next to nothing about the feminist with the acrid tongue and the sharp turn of humour, yet he found it hard to suspect her of any kind of law-breaking. He cancelled Hilda Markham as a likely suspect.

The second robbery certainly minimised the possibility of Logan and an outside accomplice being guilty – that meant that the only suspect inside the house was Cecilie.

The thief must have been in a position to see Armitage go out.

Had Cecilie been in that position?

Mannering felt gloomy as he walked towards the village. It occurred to him that Vere and Morency might be taking the footpath across the fields, in which case he would miss them. He turned, and cut across the meadow.

Presently the trees became thick and obscuring. Enjoying the cool restfulness, Mannering suddenly heard a man's voice.

He paused, for there was a threatening note in the voice which he did not like.

'It isn't all right, see,' it said. 'Don't get *that* idea. It's a long way from being all right, and you've got to see me clear. You know what'll happen if you don't.'

'But – '

A woman started to answer, and the single word sent a shock of surprise through Mannering. He had believed Lady Usk to be in her room, but there she was on the other side of the hedge of trees.

Mannering kept quite still, searching for a gap in the foliage through which he could see. He heard Lady Usk's heavy breathing, lessening in sound as she moved away towards Vere house.

But Mannering was less interested in Lady Usk than in the man who was left standing by the trees.

The thin twisted face, the sneering expression, were unmistakable. It was the man he believed to be Woolf, who had been talking to Logan and who had thrown a stone at him on the previous night.

*   *   *

Mannering stood quite still, trying to decide his wisest course of action. He could tackle the fellow at once, but would it serve any useful purpose? Would he be able to prove that it was the man whom he had seen the previous night? One man's word against another's would be of little use for a jury.

Would it damage Mannering's prospects if he identified the detective? To Mannering this man's only usefulness would be as a means of getting at the truth of the theft. If Bristow held him for any reason Mannering would have no chance of using him.

Until the thief was found Mannering had to work alone.

Then suddenly, unexpectedly, Woolf – if it was Woolf – looked round and saw Mannering.

There was no sign of recognition in the small brown eyes as the other stepped straight towards him. To reach the road he had to, for there was a stile near Mannering – the stile where Mannering had seen Logan and this fellow talking.

The man started to climb, while Mannering was still trying to reach a decision. A dozen thoughts flashed through his mind, the most convincing being that whatever he said, he would not be able to get the other to admit that he had been uttering threats. Lady Usk *could* corroborate – but would she? If she were frightened she would be far more likely to deny all knowledge of the conversation.

'Seen enough?' The coarse voice jibed.

Mannering said: 'I've seen and heard enough, I think, Woolf.' He waited long enough to see the sneer disappear and alarm enter the other's eyes. He had been right, then. This *was* Woolf.

Mannering turned away, while the other walked sharply in the opposite direction.

Had he taken the right course, Mannering wondered? As he saw it, the chief problem was whether there was any connection between this interview and the jewel robbery.

'We'll see,' Mannering said to himself. 'I fancy I'll be able to find him when I want him – and if I want him.' He stepped out briskly, and then a movement on his left attracted him. He looked round, to see Tring walking along the road. Plainly the sergeant had been hiding behind the hedge, and now he was hot-foot in Woolf's wake.

Mannering walked on, intercepting Vere and Morency halfway to the house. Both men stopped as he hailed them.

'Where's Lorna?' Vere asked when Mannering drew up. Morency smiled.

'I'm a great admirer of Miss Fauntley's painting,' he said pleasantly. 'I didn't connect her up with it last night.'

Mannering said absently, 'Few people do.' He waited a minute, and then went on. 'I'm here, really, to break a piece of tiresome news. Armitage has had his room rifled.'

Morency uttered a sharp exclamation, while Vere cried furiously:

'Another blasted robbery! Damn it, John – ' He stopped with an obvious effort to retain his composure. 'Well, all we can hope is, that Bristow can prove it was someone from outside.'

'It's pretty clear now that it wasn't,' said Mannering.

They began to walk briskly towards the house.

Morency said mildly:

'Blaming me over-much, Martin?'

'Nonsense,' answered his brother-in-law sharply. 'Only too glad to be able to help, but why this had to happen beggars me. I wonder what Bristow will do next?'

Morency said quietly: 'I don't think there's much doubt.'

'About what?' asked Mannering.

'About his course of action,' said Morency. 'We just can't have a thief in the house for this weekend. It looks as if everyone except the family will be asked to go.'

'Well,' said Mannering, 'that's understandable, and there are hotels if we don't want to go back to town.'

The luncheon gong was echoing from the house, and they hurried to their rooms. Mannering was washing his hands when Lorna came in from the passage. She was frowning, and her expression was thoughtful.

'Well, darling. What's the report?'

'Not what I want it to be,' Lorna said. 'Bristow's reached the same conclusion that we have, I'm afraid.'

'Hm-hm.'

'Cecilie's the only one of the suspects who could have taken the money from Armitage's safe,' Lorna went on, sitting down on the edge of the bath. 'She was in her room all the time – or so she says. Lady Usk was out, so was Tommy, and Hilda Markham was with Diana.'

Mannering groped for a towel.

'If we accept the obvious, then, Cecilie's the culprit. Bristow's not going to do anything about it yet, is he?'

'I don't know. He's been on the telephone in Martin's study for the last quarter of an hour.'

'Consulting with the Yard, obviously,' said Mannering. 'Well, what did you think of Cecilie?'

Lorna shrugged helplessly. 'If it weren't that so much points to her, I'd say any suspicion was absurd. She *might* have been tempted to take something from her stepmother's safe, I suppose. She was telling me that her allowance is so small that she can hardly manage. She's bitter too. But as for snooping round the rooms and taking Tommy's loose cash – I just can't believe it.'

'Morency and Vere think we'll all be asked to go until the conference is over,' said Mannering. 'And that means driving back to town after lunch or putting up in the village. Or we might go to Winchester,' he added, slipping into his coat. 'Sweetheart, if he does arrest Cecilie what are we going to do?'

'I don't know,' said Lorna. 'Would you take it for granted that she put the necklace in your room?'

Mannering said: 'I think I should want to satisfy myself that no one else could have done it. The two robberies don't worry me – but for Logan I wouldn't give a damn. But the odds and ends, the men in the grounds, the hush-hush business about Morency and the visitors this afternoon, and above all the fear of Lady Usk, are all unexplained. There's something here we haven't discovered.' Mannering hesitated as, together, they stepped towards the door. 'It might be that we're more aware of Morency's visit than we think. We're war-conscious, and he's been boosted as a messenger of peace so much that we're prepared to believe it. Do you feel that way?'

Lorna said: 'There's certainly an atmosphere.'

'An aura of unease and disquiet,' Mannering said ruminatively, 'much more so than the loss of Lady Usk's diamonds warrants. It's' – he hesitated, and then laughed without much humour – 'as if we're waiting for a crisis.'

They reached the landing, and as they did so, Mannering saw the door of Lady Usk's room opening. He looked away, not wanting to let the peeress think that he was showing too keen an interest, but he had not reached the stairs before she called him.

'Mr Mannering!'

In Lady Usk's voice there was a note that alarmed him, and startled Lorna. Mannering had heard something similar the night before, when she had cried out before she had fainted. It was more intense now, as if she were trying to shout and yet could hardly make a sound.

CHAPTER 14

And She Capitulates

Lady Usk was half-in and half-out of her room, her face ghastly beneath its make-up. Mannering stepped quickly towards her.

She was trembling, and he saw the beads of sweat on her forehead. He took her arm firmly, and led her back into the room. Lorna followed, and closed the door. Mannering urged the older woman into a chair.

'What is it, Lady Usk? What's disturbed you?'

Lady Usk was gulping for breath, but in a few seconds she grew steadier.

'I – I'm so – *frightened*.' She closed her eyes, and her fingers gripped Mannering's wrist with nervous tension. 'I –'

As she paused, Mannering said:

'Is it about the man you were talking to half-an-hour ago?'

'You mean Woolf? No, it wasn't him. He's unimportant, the fool!' Her voice strengthened, as it always did when she was contemptuous of anything or anyone, and Mannering was surprised for she had stumbled away from Woolf in a way which had suggested she was very close to panic. 'No, it was – I've had another one!'

'Another note?'

'Yes, yes! It came this morning! I didn't open the post early, I had to go and see Woolf. And when I came back – ' Her fingers fumbled at the neck of her dress, and she drew the purse out. 'See – I'm not dreaming, I'm not lying! See, there it is!'

Mannering smoothed out the small folded piece of paper she thrust into his hands and read the pencilled message:

*It won't be long now, you
old devil. You can look for
it any time.*

She allowed Mannering hardly time to read the note
before she snatched it back.

'I – I don't really mind, it's a lot of nonsense, but – ' She
shuddered. 'Who sends them, Mr Mannering? Who wants
to worry the life out of a wretched woman who hasn't done
anything to deserve it!'

'If you had,' said Mannering, 'it wouldn't justify this,
Lady Usk. I've got to advise you, very strongly, to tell the
police.'

She started up in her chair.

'No, no, I won't! And you promised not to!'

'I know I promised,' said Mannering evenly, 'but you're
taking risks, and only the police can really help you. There's
a good man in the house now.'

'I won't see him again! He was here asking all kinds of
silly questions, anyone would think he thought I'd robbed
myself!' Her voice grew strident. 'I won't tell him!'

Mannering shrugged.

'All right, you won't. But if anything happens, you probably won't be alive to regret it. I will.'

He looked sharply into the wide-open, frightened eyes as
she threw Mannering's hand aside.

'And I thought you were a friend! I tell you I'm not
really worried! I want to know who it is, that's all.'

'All right,' said Mannering. He turned to the door, but
before he reached it Lady Usk called sharply:

'Mr Mannering!'

'Yes?'

'Do you – do you really think I'm in danger?'

'It looks like it,' Mannering said. 'For myself, I wouldn't
like to be in your position.'

'And – and this policeman won't talk, will he?'

'Talk to whom?' asked Mannering with a show of irritation. 'He'll tell his superiors, and make his report, but it will
be quite confidential. He won't tell Mr and Mrs Vere or the

guests, if that's what you mean.'

Her next words startled him.

'Will – will he tell my husband?'

Mannering turned back and said reassuringly:

'It will be entirely between you and the Inspector if you decide to tell him, Lady Usk. No one, not even your husband, need know if you insist on him keeping silent about it. And I do most strongly advise you to tell Bristow.'

'All right.' She capitulated, but there was a catch in her breath. 'I'll tell him. Could he come now? Or – could *you* tell him, Mr Mannering? He's a friend of yours, isn't he?'

'He'll want to see you, and the messages,' Mannering said, 'but I'll have a word with him right away. Will you stay here until he comes along?'

'Yes. I'm having lunch up here. Yes, tell him now, please.' Lady Usk's eyes, so large and velvety, were over bright as she gripped the arms of her chair.

Outside the door, Mannering hesitated. 'She worries me, Lorna. I think you'd better wait with her until Bristow comes.'

He hurried to the study, where he found Bristow sitting at Vere's desk. Tring was standing by his side. The Inspector had a pencil and paper, but he was not writing.

Mannering walked quickly across the room. 'I've just come from Lady Usk,' he said crisply. 'She told me something yesterday, but swore me to silence. I've persuaded her that you'll treat anything she says in confidence. That's all right, I take it?'

'Of course,' said Bristow, showing a deeper interest. 'What is it?'

'Threats, on her life,' said Mannering. 'She's had two notes – the second this morning. She's in her room with Miss Fauntley now. You'd better go along while she's in the mood for talking.'

Bristow leaped to his feet.

'I appreciate this a lot, Mannering.' He paused, with his hand on the handle. 'Oh, there's one other thing. I've had instructions from London, and I'm afraid it might upset your arrangements.'

'That won't worry me,' Mannering said. 'We're all to get marching orders, I suppose.'

Bristow smiled. 'Not at all. We're asking everyone here last night to stay indefinitely. At least until Mr Morency's gone back.'

'Well,' said Mannering, 'no one will object to that. I think they were all planning to be here.'

Bristow chuckled.

'Oh, no, they weren't. Armitage wants to go to London on Monday, Miss Grey thought of going up with him, and Miss Markham changed her plans and was going back this evening. However, I'm glad you're not going to complain,' said Bristow heartily. 'Now I'll go and relieve Miss Fauntley.'

Mannering followed him out, waiting on the landing for Lorna. He was startled by the facts Bristow had thrown with a casualness too studied to be genuine. Bristow had been hoping to see some reaction to his information.

Mannering was surprised more by the several requests to leave Vere House for London than by Bristow's instructions. Obviously the authorities had decided it was better to keep the suspects in the house than let them separate; certainly they would be easier to watch. To Mannering, too, it seemed plain that the decision was controlled in a measure by Morency and the afternoon's guests. No one could carry information of whom Morency was seeing while they remained at the house.

At the same moment Cecilie's door opened and the girl stepped out. She was pale and her eyes were glittering with temper.

'Trouble?' he asked.

'Trouble?' retorted Cecilie fiercely. 'It's outrageous! I wanted to go to London, and I'm not allowed to. When I try to telephone the friend I was going to see, someone on the switchboard asks me for the message!'

Mannering himself was surprised at such highhanded treatment. It suggested that no one was to be allowed to leave, nor to telephone from Vere House. Bristow, supported by Scotland Yard and possibly the Home Office, was sealing

the house against the escape of the thief, the jewels – or—
of information.

More likely the last, Mannering thought grimly. The
impression of an approaching crisis strengthened, and grew
more urgent in his mind. Certainly this step would be
excessive but for Morency: which meant that there were
others than Wrexford to fear.

CHAPTER 15

Visitors Arrive

'I'm not coming in to lunch,' Cecilie said. 'I feel too furious!' She gave a sharp little laugh, and would have hurried past, had Lorna not stopped her.

'Don't be an idiot! We're all in the same boat. John and I have just been asked not to leave the house.'

Cecilie turned, staring incredulously.

'You two? Why?'

'For the same reasons as you,' said Mannering equably. 'There's someone in the house who doesn't object to opening safes, and during the weekend papers will be here, and things will be discussed, which could have a greater value than diamonds.'

'I don't see the connection,' Cecilie said.

'You would if you tried,' said Mannering cheerfully. 'If a man will take money and jewels he might take anything he can sell. The police mustn't take risks, and whether there had been robberies or not we would have been asked not to get in touch with anyone in town – or elsewhere,' he added, taking her elbow and guiding her towards the diningroom.

Cecilie looked slightly mollified. 'If that's the case, and the visits are so important, why don't they go somewhere else now?'

'Somewhere else could cause talk,' said Mannering. 'Anyone who learns Morency is at his sister's house sees it in a normal enough visit, and there's no apparent association with politics. None of which need concern you, Cecilie. *Do* lose the notion that you're being singled out for special notice by Bristow.'

They found Diana in the diningroom, and Hilda Markham, Vere, Morency, Armitage and Dryden. Dryden was sitting away from the others, looking intently out of the window as if searching for inspiration in the sunswept lawns and gardens. Diana was talking animatedly to Tommy. She appeared to Mannering to be too talkative – and nervous. Suddenly Hilda Markham's voice broke sharply across Diana's words.

'Di, don't try to pull the wool over our eyes, *please*. Even I can tell there's something the matter, and when the police ask us not to leave the grounds, nor telephone unless it's urgent, it's obvious that it's not all to do with Vicky. After all,' she added, in a reasoning voice, 'he's not as important as all that.'

'Thick soup or clear, Miss,' Ransome was saying imperturbably to Lorna.

'Clear, please.'

'And for me,' said Cecilie.

Unabashed by unspoken criticism, Hilda ploughed on. 'The point is, has a citizen rights of freedom and movement, or hasn't he? If Di or Martin had asked me in confidence, to stay, I would have joined the conspiracy and thought no more about it. But that Inspector Bristow –' She grimaced.

Mannering said banteringly, 'Perhaps you haven't heard that extraordinarily original saying that's going about? No, I can see you haven't.'

'And what's that,' said Hilda Markham, rubbing her spectacles vigorously.

'Why that there's a war on.'

There was a general laugh, and under cover of it Hilda leaned forward and murmured to Diana:

'Sorry, dear, I never have been noted for tact. But that Bristow man did rather get me on edge.'

Harmony was restored, but beneath the surface there remained an unpleasant awareness of things that were not understood. Even Dryden seemed to have sensed it. He was the first to leave the table.

Armitage, Morency and Vere stayed behind with Mannering, Armitage smiled.

'Hilda does put her foot in it, doesn't she?'

'She means well, but she's got a skin like a hide,' Vere assured them. He blinked at Mannering. 'That policeman fellow. Rather a decent chap, I thought.'

'There's nothing wrong with Bristow,' said Mannering, 'unless it's too keen a devotion to routine. But he's got us nicely where he wants us. Are questions taboo?'

Morency looked up with a smile.

'Answers might be.'

'Would the precautions have been quite so stringent if it weren't for the robberies?' said Mannering wonderingly.

'Well.' Morency pursed his lips. 'I don't think so, Mannering, but I can't be sure. It's your country! You three know that I was to come here on a family visit, and the other callers were to be quite casual. It didn't work out that way.'

'Personally I'm getting a kick out of it, well worth what I've lost,' Tommy said, 'although I'd like those studs back. But doesn't it seem a bit silly trying to keep things from Hilda and Dryden?'

It was another of his unexpectedly shrewd remarks, and Mannering regarded him contemplatively, wondering how much he knew, and how much he suspected. That there was more depth to the man than most people realised grew increasingly clear.

'It's up to Bristow.' Vere shrugged. 'I've no say in it. And now I'm going to have a nap. I won't last the strain if I don't.' He smiled and pushed his chair back, while the other walked across the hall to the drawing-room.

Mannering had expected Bristow to call for him after his talk with Lady Usk, but it appeared that the Yard man was determined to keep all he learned to himself.

That Bristow was deliberately holding off from Logan was plain, and confirmed Mannering's suspicion that the policeman's policy was to allow Logan plenty of rope. It gave Mannering time, but once Bristow made a thorough interrogation, the story of the necklace would surely come out.

'Do you always sleep with your eyes open?' Armitage asked impishly, 'or are you just not listening?'

Mannering brought himself up with a jerk.

'I wasn't listening,' he admitted amiably. 'It probably wasn't worth hearing, anyhow.'

'After that,' said Tommy severely, 'I'm going upstairs. Head's aching a bit,' he added, 'and Martin's idea of a nap is a good one.'

Tommy went out, and Morency, both hands deep in his pockets, looked down on Mannering, who was lounging back in an armchair.

'Armitage can't be quite what he appears, surely?'

Mannering said lazily: 'Few people are. But don't make the mistake of thinking he's not all there.'

Morency regarded Mannering with his eyes half-narrowed and his lips pursed. 'Say, if you had something that you wanted to keep really safe would you give it to Bristow?'

Mannering considered for a moment, then said:

'In the circumstances it might be wisest. Someone seems to be able to open the smaller safes. But there is a strong-room here, you know.'

Morency eyed him oddly.

'That may be, Mannering, but you're forgetting one thing. There are keys to a strong-room. That someone might' – Morency hesitated, and then went on slowly – 'might be able to get past any guard without raising suspicion. I mustn't take any chance,' he continued. '*Any* chances. Maybe I had better talk to Bristow. It might be as well that he doesn't know I asked you,' he added.

Mannering smiled grimly. 'If any man here is reliable, Bristow is.'

'You know him,' Morency said. 'But *is* any man reliable? I've been double-crossed before now by men I'd stake my life on.' He shrugged and went towards the door, but it opened before he reached it. Mannering saw Bristow, and the overhanging fear that Logan had talked returned.

'Ah, Mr Mannering.' There was no informality about Bristow unless they were alone. 'Can you spare me ten minutes?'

'When you like,' said Mannering, but his heart thudded.

'And when you've finished,' said Morency, 'I'd like a word with you, Inspector.'

Bristow looked at him sharply.

'I'm at your service, sir. Mr Mannering won't mind waiting, I'm sure.'

'Ten minutes will make no difference,' said Morency. 'I'll be in the study, if you'll be good enough to come up.'

Bristow looked at the closing door before he turned to Mannering. There was no hint of a threat in his manner.

'I've had a long talk with Lady Usk,' he said. 'Apart from these two notes, she says that she knows nothing. But to me, it doesn't ring true. Did she tell you anything more?'

'Nothing more at all.'

'Blast the woman!' exclaimed Bristow. 'It's a complication I didn't want. How has the general order been taken?' he added with a smile.

'Reasonably well,' said Mannering. 'The ban on the telephone calls hasn't been appreciated by everyone.'

'It was unavoidable,' said Bristow. He hesitated. 'Do you know who's coming?'

Mannering shook his head, trying not to show his interest.

'The Chancellor of the Exchequer, and Sir Eustace Defoe.' Bristow paused to study the effect of his words but he had little satisfaction, for Mannering made no comment. Bristow smiled grimly. 'They're coming alone, thank God – except for secretaries. With Usk and Deverell that will be the lot. I'll bet from now until Tuesday morning will be the longest weekend I've ever lived through.'

Mannering stiffened.

'Now what's the matter?' Bristow demanded suspiciously.

Mannering said slowly: 'I thought the Usks and the Deverells were a long way from being friends. What's bringing Deverell?'

'I don't know,' said Bristow, 'but there was a wire just before lunch. He's expected in the next half-hour or so. Probably he didn't know who else was here, but why should there be anything between him and Lord Usk?'

Mannering said: 'It's well known that they're not on speaking terms.' He shrugged. 'I certainly agree with you that it's likely to be a long weekend, I haven't much doubt of that.'

Both men looked out of the window at a car turning into the drive. Bristow moved to the door at once.

'Well, keep your eyes open, and if you get a chance of finding out what's worrying Miss Grey I wouldn't be sorry to know.' He disappeared.

Mannering, continuing to stare out of the window, saw the short, square-shouldered figure of the Chancellor of the Exchequer step from a Rolls. He walked briskly up the steps, followed by Lord Marle and the Honourable Richard Grayson, both parliamentary under-secretaries. The car was driven away but was followed within a few minutes by a Daimler, and Sir Eustace Defoe, Governor of the Bank of England, followed in Gresham's steps.

That left Usk and Deverell to come, thought Mannering, and as he turned from the window he wondered again why Deverell had chosen that weekend to visit the Veres, whether there would be trouble between him and Lady Usk.

Did he know the Usks would be present?

Mannering shrugged, but felt uneasy. The silence upstairs did nothing to relieve the feeling of disquiet. Lorna was not in her room, and Cecilie was also out. Armitage was missing – he had not gone to rest, for Mannering could see him on the putting green not far from Mannering's window.

Ten minutes later Armitage tapped on his door, and came in boisterously.

'I say, old man, this is the utter last word! Usk's arrived – you'll never guess who else!'

'Deverell,' said Mannering.

'How the devil did – ' Armitage stared blankly, and then went on with a grin: 'There you go, criminologising again. They came up the drive together, or nearly together. I thought Usk would drop dead when he saw Deverell climbing out on his heels. John, my son, this is going to be a weekend of weekends, and we're in the stalls!'

'Yes,' said Mannering slowly. 'I'm not sure that I don't wish I were somewhere else.'

'Gloomy old kill-joy,' said Armitage lightly. 'I'm all for

fire-works. Care for a spot of tennis?'

'With that hole in your head I wouldn't take the responsibility,' said Mannering. 'Shouldn't you be resting?'

'Not now,' said Armitage. 'I might miss something. See you later, then. By the way, where's Cecilie? I can't find her.'

'Somewhere with Lorna I think,' said Mannering.

He gazed pensively after Armitage's back. Was his curiosity as naive as it appeared?

Mannering sat back concentrating on the new situation created by the arrival of Usk and Deverell. He had been alone for ten minutes when he heard a door bang with such violence that it made him start. A shout followed. He stepped swiftly to the passage.

He saw Lady Usk stepping towards the staircase, her face blazing and her hands clenched. She staggered against the balustrade, and Mannering thought she would fall. But she recovered and went unsteadily downstairs.

Mannering followed.

When he reached the landing he saw that her door was now open, and Usk was framed in it. On the Irish peer's face there was an expression of such malevolence that Mannering was appalled.

The hint which Cecilie had given him, and Lady Usk's insistence that her husband should know nothing of her approach to the police, combined to show the fear which Usk caused his wife – a fear at least as great as that inspired by the pencilled notes.

It was obvious to Mannering that Usk hated his wife; but had he threatened her?

Chapter 16
Enter Death

Whatever the feelings of those guests who had been at the house before the new arrivals, there was no outward sign of dissension or anxiety. Neither Defoe nor Gresham appeared at tea, and Morency was also missing. Their secretaries were in the drawing-room, however, and of the others only Lady Usk kept to her room. There was a stiffness between Deverell and Usk which was not too noticeable.

It would have been hard to meet two more dissimilar men.

There was a burly heartiness about Mike Deverell which was reminiscent of Tommy Armitage. A man of forty-odd, he would have passed easily for thirty-five, while his youthful manner aided the deception. Mannering knew that he was on the Reserve of Officers, but after being called up in the early days of the war had been sent back for no apparent reason; when Mannering had last seen him he had been complaining bitterly about the red tape. Mannering, in a similar position, had been able to sympathise.

Financially the war had hit Deverell badly, and his wife was well-known for her extravagance – hence the sale of the necklace. But it was impossible to detect any sign of grievance or worry in Deverell's bluff countenance, and his blue eyes were friendly and smiling.

Usk was twenty years older, a small, wizened man with a Van Dyck beard. A colourless man, too, about whom little was known except that he had mended the family fortunes by marrying into millions, and that he specialised in revolver shooting. His manner, quick and abrupt, Mannering attributed to nerves.

Deverell singled Mannering out.

'Well, John, I'm glad to find you here. Are you staying long?'

'For a few days,' said Mannering. 'And you?'

Deverell smiled. 'I felt like a weekend, and Di's always ready to take pity on me. Elsie's in Miami, but I'm damned if I'll sun myself these days.' It was the only reference he made to his wife, but Mannering felt that all was not well between them.

'I – hallo, there's Di calling, I'd better go. Funny how we all eat out of her hand, isn't it? By the way, who's the little woman with a sharp tongue?'

'Hilda Markham,' Mannering informed him. 'Economics is her line, but she *can* laugh.'

'I don't believe it,' said Deverell. 'See you later.'

It was not until dinner that the whole party re-assembled. Gresham and Defoe had brought five secretaries with them, so that the women were outnumbered by nearly four to one.

Talk ebbed and flowed, and there was little sign of strain, although the two men from London doggedly stuck to trivialities, blandly ignoring Armitage's eager, hopeful expression.

Mannering touched his arm.

'Forgotten your specs, Tommy?'

'Don't be a mug,' said Tommy, but he coloured a little. 'I can't help feeling that we're watching history, and all that kind of thing. Hasn't it got you yet?'

'No,' said Mannering, 'and if you're not careful it will get you into difficulties. Everyone here is doing a mighty best to make it seem an informal weekend party.'

'All right, I get the point,' said Tommy huffily. He was silent for some minutes, but soon his bandaged head moved towards Mannering. 'Dare I talk about the Usk?

'What about her?'

'I didn't mean her, I meant him. Sour-visaged old beggar, isn't he? Living with *that* by day and night would make anyone screech. For the first time I'm sorry for Lady U.' Tommy glanced across the table.

There was – as so often happened – something in Armitage's suggestion. Usk was a man who could easily frighten; and Lady Usk *was* frightened.

Her step-daughter, Mannering noticed, appeared to be at her vivacious best. Defoe's secretaries were on either side of her, and although neither was young, Cecilie was obviously enjoying their attentions. A striking contrast to the silent, too-colourful face of Lady Usk, who sat, grim and expressionless, as if the events of the past day had aged her beyond recovery.

As the ladies left the room, Mannering wondered whether Cecilie would go into the grounds again. No mention was made by the remaining men, of the robberies, nor of the political visitors. The usual jokes passed across the table, while Tommy's laugh grew longer and louder. Nevertheless, Mannering noticed that he drank very little; perhaps because of Dr Brill's orders.

When they went into the drawing-room, they all joined easily enough into the general chatter. Presently Lady Usk stood up and went out of the door leading to the front hall. Mannering saw Cecilie glance towards her, and Cecilie's expression was difficult to understand.

The girl murmured something to her companions, and followed her step-mother.

Lord Usk and Gresham were talking, but Deverell's eyes followed the movements of the older woman, his expression inscrutable.

Mannering leaned towards Lorna.

'I'm slipping out for a moment,' he said. 'Make sure who stays in the room, will you?'

She nodded, and he went into the front hall, slipping quietly through to the garden.

It was as dark as on the previous night, but now sultry and oppressive; a storm was likely to break before long.

In the distance a flash of lightning sent a white streak across the sky. Before it faded however, Mannering saw fleetingly the upright figure of a man.

His heart beat faster.

It might be one of Bristow's men, but there was an equal chance that it was one of the prowlers of the previous night.

He waited for the next flash, but when it came the man had moved under cover of some bushes nearby: Mannering caught only a glimpse of him before he was out of sight. Then the silence was about him again, and the darkness – both to be broken when the front door opened.

Mannering held his breath.

The footsteps on the porch were too heavy for Cecilie. He peered closer, and caught the gleam of a white bandage.

Armitage!

Was he curious too, or was he here on business not yet known to Mannering?

Armitage stepped along the drive, and then his footsteps ceased. He had reached the grass verge, and it was impossible to tell whether he was watching the house or moving away from it. Mannering resisted the temptation to follow him, and was glad a few minutes afterwards, for the door opened again and he saw Cecilie. She closed the door softly, and then walked in Armitage's wake, using a torch which shed a clear circle of light.

Mannering went after her.

Halfway along the drive she stopped. Into the radius of torch light stepped a man whose thin, twisted features were clear enough to Mannering.

It was Woolf.

Mannering drew nearer. Another flash of lightning lit up the garden, and by it Mannering saw others; Bristow, quite close to Cecilie and Woolf, and Tring not far away; and also a motionless, unrecognisable man further along the drive.

There was no sign of Armitage's bandaged head.

Could the motionless man be Logan?

Darkness fell about them again like a shroud.

Mannering felt his pulse beating fast. The police, the mysterious unknown, Cecilie and Woolf on business that might be connected with the jewel robbery, Armitage somewhere nearby, and himself waiting and watching – and perhaps being watched by others beside Bristow.

The only light now, was that cast by Cecilie's torch. The ghostly white circle added to the eeriness of waiting.

Suddenly Woolf's voice came sharp and clear. 'I've had enough, see? I'm through! You'll either –'

A dull peal of thunder, unexpectedly close, drowned his words.

Mannering was five yards from Cecilie, and Woolf was talking again, when he heard the shot.

Exaggerated by the silence, it crashed about his ears, and its echoes were still ringing when Woolf staggered. The light from Cecilie's torch showed the man's lips parted with sudden pain.

Then Cecilie turned and ran towards the house.

The grounds suddenly awakened to life and sound.

Three torches stabbed through the gloom, two of them with almost a searchlight brilliance. Footsteps sounded on the gravel, crashing through the bushes and undergrowth.

Cecilie's flying figure drew close to Mannering.

He shot out a hand, grabbing at her coat.

'Don't run away, you little idiot!'

'John!'

'Yes,' said Mannering, 'but don't talk. Three or four people know you've been out, but you're about the only one here who can't be suspected of the shooting. Come with me.'

He hurried towards the spot where Woolf had fallen. Cecilie followed, her breathing harsh and uneven.

Mannering was the first to reach Woolf. He went on his knees beside the man, carefully seeking for the pulse; but he found no flicker of movement. Body and features were distorted in death.

Cecilie said in a strained voice: 'He – he's dead, isn't he?'

'I can't be sure,' Mannering said. As he straightened up he murmured urgently: 'I'm not interested in why you came out to meet him, but I am interested in what you tell the police. Don't lie. If you don't want to answer any questions you needn't, but what you do say must be the truth. And don't pretend you met him by accident, or say that you merely came out for a breathe of air. Is that clear?'

'Yes.'

'For God's sake act on it,' said Mannering, and then he turned to face the light from Sergeant Tring's torch.

'Hallo, Tring. You didn't take long to get here.'

'No, sir,' said Tring. He, too, went down on his knees beside Woolf. Mannering heard his sharp intake of breath, but before the detective sergeant made any comment, the engine of a car started up from somewhere not far off.

There was a high-powered whine as it was revved too quickly: then the engine picked up and the noise grew further away.

Was the gunman in it?

Mannering spent little time pondering the question, for footsteps could be heard coming briskly along the drive, and almost at once Bristow was revealed in the light of Tring's torch. He said sharply:

'Cut in for Anderson, Tring, and everything we need. Now, Mr Mannering, what can you tell me about this?'

'No more than you already know,' Mannering said.

'Hmm. Miss Grey.' It was impossible to see Bristow's expression, but his voice was forbidding. 'Do you know who this man is?'

Cecilie said: 'His – his name's Woolf.'

'What did you want with him?'

'I think,' said Mannering easily, 'that it's a bad moment for asking questions, Inspector. Miss Grey has had a shock. I can testify to the fact, that she did not shoot him.'

'I suggested nothing of the kind,' retorted Bristow. 'Miss Grey, it will be wiser for you to answer questions now.'

Mannering said easily:

'I'm sure Miss Grey will answer anything you want to ask her in the house, Inspector. We can't stay here. The storm will be on us in a matter of minutes.'

As he spoke, a clap of thunder, louder than the previous ones, reverberated above them. Suddenly the rain began to fall in earnest, pelting down with a tropical intensity. Mannering gave Cecilie a light push towards the house.

'Run for it, Cecilie! Can I give you a hand, Bristow?'

Bristow was forced to make the best of it. He grunted his acquiescence, and between them they carried the body towards the house. By the time they reached it they were wet through. In the hall the water streamed from them, making little pools on the carpet. Ransome stood by the open door, expressionless and awaiting orders. The drawing-room door opened, and Martin Vere came through.

'Good God!' he exclaimed. 'What's this?'

Bristow said sharply: 'Is there a small room where we can take the man?'

'Of course.' Vere blinked at Mannering, glancing quickly away from the distorted face of the dead man. 'Ransome, the morning room will be the best, I think.'

Before they reached it footsteps came rapidly down the stairs, and Tommy Armitage hurried towards them, his face alive with excitement.

'What on earth's been happening now? I fancied I heard a shot, and was just coming out. I – oh, Lord!' He broke off as he saw Woolf's face, and he too, turned abruptly away. 'Just as well I didn't come out, eh?'

No one answered him, but Mannering felt a shock that was not altogether of surprise. Armitage was intimating that he had not been outside. Why had he decided to lie?

Chapter 17

Some Are Clear

'Oh, Mannering,' Bristow said. 'I'd like a word with you.'

Mannering nodded.

Little time had been lost, and Dr Brill was on the way to the house, though he could do no more than confirm that death had been caused by a bullet wound in the back.

Cecilie was in her room, and Lorna and a detective were with her. Bristow had no intention of letting her talk to Mannering or Lorna unattended, and Mannering could not blame the man. He was relieved only by one thing – that Cecilie certainly had not fired the shot.

Now Mannering followed Bristow to his room on the second floor. Bristow pointed to an easy chair, while he himself sat at the table, fingering his moustache and looking hard at Mannering.

'Well,' said Mannering. 'What now?'

'I'm not sure,' said Bristow slowly. 'There's one thing that must be made quite clear, Mannering, before we go any further. You are not to interfere with the work of the police. What questions we ask and how we ask them are no business of yours.'

Mannering demurred. 'I can't grant you that. If a friend of mine is in need of help, he or she gets it. The girl had had a shock, and she hardly knew what she was saying. You came perilously near to brow-beating her.'

'Nonsense,' said Bristow sourly. 'Tring tells me you talked to her before he reached you. What did you say?'

'I advised her to tell nothing but the truth,' said Mannering.

'That's likely,' sneered Bristow.

'Likely or not, it's a fact.' Mannering sank more deeply in his chair. 'I was out before Miss Grey, and I went out because I wanted to know if anyone left the house again tonight. She did, of course. You saw her talking to Woolf, and you saw just as much as I did. You saw who came out.'

'Don't hint,' Bristow said. 'Yes, I saw Mr Armitage.'

'All right,' said Mannering. 'You know Miss Grey didn't shoot Woolf, and you know I didn't. That's right, isn't it?'

'Yes,' said Bristow, but he sounded reluctant to make the admission.

'Fine,' said Mannering. 'Of the murder, then, both Miss Grey and I are quite clear. I've a feeling,' he added ingenuously, 'that your man got away.'

'I'm not interested in your feelings,' said Bristow sharply. 'Someone drove off, but it wasn't necessarily the murderer. Mannering, have you any idea why Woolf was killed?'

'None at all.'

'Was he threatening Miss Grey?'

'I heard what you must have heard, and no more.'

'Had you seen the man before?'

'Well, yes. I was coming to that. I've seen him several times. First, on Friday afternoon – yesterday – talking to Lady Usk's chauffeur. Again last light; he was the man I chased through the grounds.'

Bristow leaned forward. 'Was he, by Jove! You didn't tell me you'd recognised him.'

'No,' said Mannering. 'I couldn't be absolutely sure then, though I can now. And this morning,' he added easily, 'I saw him talking to Lady Usk.'

'You're sure of that?'

'Quite sure.'

'What were they talking about?'

'I didn't hear,' said Mannering, and he had no hesitation in lying. 'But I saw Tring nearby. Didn't he get anything?'

'Go on.' Bristow was uncompromising.

'They might have met by accident, Bristow, but if you'd like my ideas about it – ' He paused.

'Go on,' said Bristow again.

'Lady Usk,' said Mannering carefully, 'hired Logan from

an Inquiry Agency called the Woolf something or other. I imagined that this fellow was connected with it, and that she was talking to him on business. She would want the interview secret. After the interview she looked badly hit. I took it that there was no news of her jewels. That appears,' added Mannering easily, 'to explain it reasonably well.'

'You don't know why she called him in?'

'I don't know any more than I told you this morning.'

There was a short silence, and then Bristow stood up abruptly.

'It's a blasted nuisance,' he snapped, 'that all these complications should turn up this weekend of all weekends. I'll be suspecting a Cabinet Minister before I go much further. Look here, Mannering – I don't want anything done without my knowing. If you feel like doing anything on your own, I strongly advise you against it.'

'Locked up here there isn't much I can do,' said Mannering.

'Well don't say I haven't warned you,' said Bristow shortly. 'I'm not having any fooling about, by you or anyone else, until after Tuesday.'

Mannering smiled. 'And I can do what I like after that?'

'You can do nothing of the kind,' said Bristow. 'And now I'm going to talk to Miss Grey. You won't be there, and nor will anyone else.'

'Well, go easy with her, Bill. Don't overplay your hand.'

'And what do you mean by that?' Bristow flashed.

'I have a feeling you might,' said Mannering easily.

'If you're keeping back information the police should have, you'll regret it.'

'All I'm keeping back,' said Mannering gently, 'is an appreciation of human nature, and Miss Grey's in particular.'

'Oh, go to blazes,' said Bristow testily. He pressed a bell behind him, and Sergeant Anderson appeared with startling suddenness. 'Anderson, bring Miss Grey up when I ring next time, and send Tring in.'

Anderson went out, but Mannering lingered.

'Bristow – did you see Logan in the grounds tonight?'

'Yes,' said Bristow. 'But he was in the house when the shooting happened. Stop interfering. I'll look after Logan in good time.'

'As you did Woolf?' Mannering asked sharply.

He went out, surprised that Logan was cleared from the shooting. Who else would want to kill Woolf? And why had Cecilie arranged that meeting?

Bristow's manner; the 'bring Miss Grey here when I ring next' had been decisive; there had been no 'ask Miss Grey to come here'.

Had Bristow more evidence than Mannering knew?

Tring knocked on the Inspector's door, and went in. Mannering hesitated, and then stepped softly back to the room. The door was closed, but words could be heard and Bristow was saying:

'You're quite sure about it?'

'I've got the prints here, sir. See . . . ' there followed a few words that were indistinguishable, and then: 'They're from the safe in Mr Armitage's room, and they're from her hairbrush. You couldn't mistake them.'

Mannering moved away swiftly, and was at the head of the stairs before Tring came out. His heart was beating fast, and his eyes were hard. The many indications that Cecilie had committed the thefts had crystallised with Tring's statement; he had been discussing fingerprints, and finding Cecilie's prints on Armitage's safe gave Bristow a strong case, perhaps an unbreakable one.

He reached Cecilie's room only a few yards ahead of Anderson.

Lorna and Cecilie looked up quickly, and Cecilie's face hardened at the sight of Anderson.

'The Inspector wants a word with you, Cecilie,' Mannering said. 'Remember, you must stick to the truth.' He gave her a reassuring smile. She smiled back again, before following Anderson out.

Lorna ran her fingers through her hair, 'What on earth does Bristow want?'

'To catch a thief and a murderer,' said Mannering quietly, 'and he's got good grounds for the arrest. Her prints were on Armitage's safe.'

'Good God!' exclaimed Lorna blankly.

'Yes, it's bad.' Mannering's expression was sombre. 'He thinks that the murder was prearranged, of course. He may be following the theory that Cecilie kept the man under a spotlight knowing that he was going to be shot.'

Lorna said: 'It can't be possible!'

'It's possible all right,' Mannering said. 'I don't know Cecilie well enough to swear that it's beyond her, but it would give me a jolt if it was proved.'

'She's certainly a little strange tonight,' said Lorna. 'I could hardly get a word out of her.'

'What do you mean by "strange"?'

'Well, defiant,' said Lorna. 'She denied nothing, and said the police could do what they liked, anything would be a relief from living with her stepmother.'

'Hmm,' Mannering said. 'There's one odd thing about this set-up. Lady Usk gets threatened, and robbed. She's the obvious victim, but it's Armitage who gets hurt, and Woolf who gets killed. I wonder – was she out of the room when the shot was fired?'

'She must have been.'

Mannering said slowly: 'Who else was out of the room?'

Lorna reflected. 'Lady Usk, one, Armitage, two, Hilda Markham, three.'

'Was she, by Jove! Had she been out long?'

'She followed Armitage.'

'Hmm. And the others?'

'Usk slipped out,' said Lorna, 'but that was only a few minutes before the thunder. I doubt whether he could have had time. And Deverell was out for quite a while.'

'We're getting a nice gallery of suspects,' said Mannering. 'It might be quicker to ask who was *in* the room.' He looked expectantly at Lorna.

'Well, Defoe and Gresham, Morency, Dryden, Vere, and Di – no, Diana had gone out. There was some talk about a bridge party.'

Mannering said: 'Except for Deverell and Usk, every one of the guests who arrived today is quite clear. Deverell and

Usk,' he ended softly, 'are two people with particular reason to dislike Lady Usk.'

'They couldn't have opened her safe.'

'Couldn't they?' asked Mannering. 'We don't know where they were last night. They could have been in the grounds, for all we know, among the prowlers. We can't count either of them out.'

'It seems absurd to think of Mike robbing anyone,' said Lorna, half-heartedly.

'They're all possibles,' Mannering insisted, 'and there are plenty for Bristow to choose from. He'll start with Cecilie, of course. I wonder if Toby Plender could come down? There's not likely to be any objection to me sending for him.'

'No,' said Lorna. 'You think she'll need legal help right away?'

'The quicker the better,' said Mannering. He felt disturbed and depressed. 'Well, now, Tommy needs some explaining. *He* was outside.'

'So I gathered,' said Lorna. 'He was so anxious to say he wasn't. Is he fond of Cecilie?'

'He gave every sign of being so,' said Mannering, 'but the stepmother frightened him off.'

'Just another reason for disliking Lady Usk,' said Lorna. 'John, is there any chance that someone not at the house killed Woolf?'

Mannering shrugged. 'A small one, but Bristow will come down heavily if I start asking too many questions. He can't stop us going downstairs,' he added, more lightly. 'Unless you'd rather wait for Cecilie?'

'I think I will,' said Lorna.

Downstairs, Mannering found that Armitage and Vere had rejoined the main party, and Hilda Markham was exchanging a rapid back-chat with Deverell.

Morency strolled over a moment later and sat next to Mannering.

'Something else has gone wrong, I guess.' His slow, unexcitable voice reached only Mannering's ears.

'Yes, but you'd better hear about it from the police,' said Mannering. 'Have you decided what to do with your valuables?' He spoke half humorously.

'I've given them to Bristow,' said Morency with a shrug. 'That should be all right. Do you play golf, Mannering?'

Mannering looked surprised. 'Yes, but I'm no great shakes.'

'Good,' said Morency. 'There'll be a golfing party tomorrow morning, weather permitting, and I've checked up now that everyone plays except Miss Markham, Vere, and—' He glanced across at Defoe and the Chancellor. 'You follow?'

Mannering smiled. 'Yes, I've got it.'

Morency, Defoe and Gresham, then, would be at the house on the next day, and the rest of the party, but for Martin and Hilda, would be playing golf. It was a good way of holding a conference without being too obvious. But why the two exceptions?

Defoe came towards them, and they changed the subject. Defoe was genial company, with a constant fund of good stories. It was hard to believe that behind his twinkling brown eyes there were the secrets of the Bank of England, and a knowledge of finance and economics probably unrivalled. It was harder to believe that Gresham was here to discuss matters which might alter the course of the war.

At that moment Vere came into the room leaving the door open.

Mannering was glad that he did, for otherwise he would not have heard the cry from upstairs. It was Cecilie calling, her voice strained and high-pitched.

'No, no, no! You can't!'

Mannering was the first out of the room. He saw Cecilie running down the stairs well ahead of Bristow, with Tring in the rear. Bristow's face was set, and he looked livid. Cecilie looked frightened out of her life – and in her hand was a small automatic which she waved wildly. She saw Mannering but did not stop her headlong flight. As she reached the hall she drew up and turned the gun towards her breast.

Mannering jumped at her.

He knocked her arm away, and the gun went flying. In

the scuffle Cecilie's face pressed against his shoulder.

'They're in my room,' she muttered hoarsely. 'The jewels – don't let the police find them, I didn't take them.'

Then she started to scream again, her cries piercing through the hall. Bristow gripped her wrist, not unkindly.

Mannering said: 'What the devil are you doing to her, Bristow?'

'I've charged her with theft,' said Bristow sharply, 'and I'll thank you not to interfere, Mr Mannering. I'm sorry, Miss Grey, but you are quite at liberty to get legal advice. If you're innocent you have nothing at all to fear.'

From his expression Mannering knew that he doubted whether she was innocent – while Mannering knew now that the jewels, which would serve as reasonable proof of her guilt, were in her room.

And – she had a gun.

CHAPTER 18

Armitage Lets Himself Go

Bristow sat back, pressing his hands against his forehead. He had wanted everything to go quietly and without fuss: instead, the whole house had been disturbed, and now there was not one of the guests who did not know that Cecilie Grey was under arrest for the robbery. Moreover he had seen the expression of sharp disapproval on the face of the Chancellor of the Exchequer, and he expected a summons to that gentleman at any moment.

Damn the girl!

It seemed an open-and-shut case against her. She had had the opportunity for the robberies, she had a motive – he knew that Lady Usk kept her stepdaughter on an allowance that was absurdly low – and she had refused to give any explanation of her meeting with Woolf, or of her walk in the grounds of the previous night. She had had the opportunity of getting at Lady Usk's purse more easily than anyone else. Up to there it was all circumstantial, Bristow acknowledged to himself, but reasonable, even if hardly strong enough to justify an arrest.

Then Anderson and Bennett, making discreet inquiries in the servant's hall, had learned that Cecilie had been seen in her stepmother's room ten minutes before Lady Usk's cry had brought Mannering and Armitage. The maids – two of them, who had been going round turning the beds down – were quite definite about it.

Bristow had at first decided to hold his hand convinced that the girl did not work alone, but the murder of Woolf had demanded quick action, and the fingerprints found on Armitage's safe decided him to act.

As Mannering suspected, Bristow saw the possibility that the girl had spot-lighted Woolf so that the murderer could shoot. Whether the actual gunman was in the house, or someone from outside, he did not know, but Bristow believed that if the girl was arrested it would start things moving. His aim was to get the robberies and murder cleared up before the Chancellor of the Exchequer, Defoe and Morency started their conversations. This, of course, had been foiled by the scene in the hall.

He writhed at the memory of it, seeing again in his mind's eye the girl as she ran screaming down the stairs, determined to cause a disturbance. And then she had banged into Mannering – and been silent for some seconds.

Bristow wondered about those seconds. How much of her screaming had been genuine, and how much had been put on for effect? For the gun had proved to be empty.

There was a tap on the door, and Anderson came in.

'Well, Anderson?'

'Mr Gresham would like to see you, sir, in the study.'

Bristow pushed his chair back. 'Who else is with him?'

'Mr Vere, sir, Mr Morency, and Sir Eustace Defoe.'

Bristow shrugged, and muttered something under his breath.

He reached the study, and tapped, feeling depressed, angry with Cecilie, and a little anxious about the reception likely to await him. He was not cheered when he saw the uncompromising face of Gresham, behind Vere's desk, Morency quite expressionless, and Defoe with lips set tightly.

'You sent for me, sir?'

'Yes, Inspector.' Gresham's voice was acid. 'I'm sorry that you found that disturbance necessary.'

'I assure you, sir,' said Bristow evenly, 'that I did everything with the utmost discretion. Miss Grey was hysterical.'

'There was surely some way of preventing a *chase*,' said Gresham. 'Do I understand that she is under arrest for the jewel-robbery?'

'On suspicion, yes, sir.'

'And on no other charge?'

'Not at the moment, sir,' said Bristow. 'There is something else which I have to report, sir. I sent a message to you – I hope you received it.'

'This is the response,' said Gresham coldly. 'What has happened tonight?'

Bristow's voice sank to the same temperature. 'Miss Grey met a man in the grounds, sir. I believed it to be in connection with the robbery, and followed her. I kept her under observation. While doing so the man was shot by someone as yet unknown.'

'*Shot!*' Defoe almost shouted the word, and Morency stood up abruptly.

'Is he badly hurt?'

'He's dead, sir.'

'Good God!' exclaimed Defoe. 'Shot under your eyes, Inspector!'

'As you know, sir,' said Bristow quietly, 'the grounds were watched, and all exits to the house are under observation. I brought six men with me for that purpose. In spite of it a man or woman entered the grounds, shot the man, and escaped. Someone also went off in a car. Whether it was the murderer or not, I can't be sure.'

'Are you telling me, Inspector' – Gresham's voice sounded dangerously quiet – 'that the murderer escaped?'

'It was impossible to prevent him, sir,' said Bristow. 'The black-out was too intense, and there was practically no light.'

Morency spoke for the first time. 'Inspector, when you say you are not sure whether the murderer was the man who went off in a car, are you suggesting that he is in the house?'

'That remains a possibility, sir.'

Defoe's voice, sharpened by anxiety, now broke in. 'Bristow, do you understand the full implications of this? With you on the premises, safes can be opened, and strangers appear in the grounds at will. You have no check, apparently, on the movements of guests and servants. At our special request you were sent down to make sure that **the weekend was not disturbed unduly by yesterday's** occurrence. You seem to have failed completely.'

'I can think of nothing I have left undone, sir. There appears to be no connection between the crimes committed here, and your visit.'

'Are you quite sure about that?' Morency asked quietly.

Gresham turned a startled eye towards the American, who went on:

'It did occur to me, gentlemen, that this might be an effort to disturb us. An atmosphere of murder and robbery is hardly conducive to amicable discussion, and none of us at the moment is feeling at his best.'

'You – think – but no, Morency, it's too far-fetched,' Defoe muttered. He took out a handkerchief and trumpeted loudly. 'I can see your point, of course, but I don't think we've anything to fear in that respect. Eh, Bristow?'

'I can only say that it is possible, sir,' said Bristow coldly. 'You know, of course, that Mr Morency is being watched.'

'Yes, yes.' Gresham's voice was sharp. 'But the two men are under your surveillance, aren't they?'

'We're watching very closely, sir,' said Bristow.

Gresham drummed his fingers on the desk.

'All right, then, Bristow. I suppose the black-out conditions do make it more difficult for you. But you're charged with seeing that all the documents brought here by us are kept safely. You understand that?'

'Just where are they?' Defoe demanded.

Vere spoke for the first time.

'In the strong-room, Defoe, I told you. You've examined it, Inspector, haven't you?'

'It would be difficult to break into,' admitted Bristow.

'But not impossible?' drawled Morency.

Bristow came near to losing patience.

'I've never known a safe or a strong-room that is impossible to force, sir. I think Sir Eustace will agree with me that given the right circumstances the vaults at the Bank of England could be entered – that's why there is a day-and-night guard. There is one here, also, and the guard is armed.'

'Guard?' asked Gresham. 'Singular, Bristow?'

'I've had a man there all day, sir, but there will be two during the night. If you would care to come down to see the precautions I'm sure you will feel satisfied.'

'I think we will,' said Defoe.

Gresham nodded, and they went downstairs together, Bristow and Vere in the lead. In the hall, Armitage and Mannering were talking. As he saw Bristow, Armitage, very red in the face, took a step towards him, but Mannering held him back.

Bristow scowled as he went along the passage by the staircase. He was grateful to Mannering for preventing Armitage from interrupting then, but he sensed that Armitage was upset by the arrest of the girl, and he wanted no more complications. He unlocked a door which led to a short flight of stone steps.

'You see,' Vere explained, 'this is the only entry. There's no other way of getting to it.' He stood aside, as Bristow unlocked an iron-studded door. He had to exert considerable force to get it open wide enough for the others to go through.

They were in a room, no more than three yards square, which was lined with safes of the most up-to-date type. The keyholes were small, but Bristow demonstrated the way in which they opened. The first door was a dummy, a sheet of steel half-an-inch thick. The second was of steel padded with asbestos, and the third showed the safe. Bristow flicked on a torch.

'Everything is there,' he said. 'Perhaps you'll confirm that, gentlemen.'

Gresham looked through the envelopes.

'Four in all – that seems all right, Bristow.'

'Had we better look inside?' Morency asked.

Defoe shrugged. 'It hardly seems necessary, but, since we're here – ' He took a knife from his pocket and slit the first envelope.

'Six safes in all,' Gresham said ruminatively. 'What is in the others, Bristow?'

'I understand that Mr Vere keeps his valuables here, sir.'

'That's right.' Vere spoke without turning round. 'Not that there's much left these days.' He laughed wryly.

'Well, Defoe, are you quite satisfied?'

'Yes,' said Defoe. 'Except – couldn't there be a man inside the vault, Vere?'

'*Inside?* I don't know, I'd never thought of it. It would get a bit stuffy after a bit, I expect. There's a ventilator, though. I had one put in ten years or so ago, after I was locked in by mistake. I thought my time had come,' he added off-handedly.

'I could put a man in, and have the door opened every half hour,' said Bristow.

'But that would mean two men here, and none watching,' said Morency.

'A third man could be watching,' said Bristow patiently.

'In that case, I think it's a good idea,' Morency said. 'You'll forgive me for being so insistent, I know. The vault by itself would be all right at normal times, but with so much happening that we cannot understand, I'd be happier if we took this added precaution.'

Bristow led the way decisively back to the hall.

'I'm glad that's arranged, gentlemen,' he said, 'and I'll see that it's put into operation at once.'

'Right you are,' said Gresham. 'Oh, Bristow – what do you propose doing with that girl? Is she staying here?'

'I don't think so, sir,' said Bristow. 'We can't lock her up in a room all night with one of the men – we can't spare a man for that anyhow, and it would give her cause for complaint. She'll be better off in Winchester.'

'Are you putting her in a cell?'

'It isn't necessary, sir, for tonight. I'll have to get in touch with London before I decide whether to ask for a first hearing in the morning. There's no Court on Sunday, so it will have to be left for a day. But in any case, I don't feel inclined to let her stay here. She might find a way of causing further disturbance.'

'That's reasonable,' said Gresham. 'Get her into Winchester then, Inspector. I wonder what the weather is like?'

He peered through the front door, but a bluster of wind sent rain spattering into the hall, and Gresham drew back and closed the door quickly.

Bristow had gone to make the arrangements. It fell to Anderson to be locked inside the strong-room, and Tring to open the strong-room at half-hour intervals. Bennett was to stay outside, hidden by a curtain.

That decided, Bristow went to Cecilie's room.

The plainclothes man with her looked uncomfortably towards his superior, and motioned to the huddled figure on the bed. Bristow's face hardened, for he was coming to the conclusion that the girl could put on a show of grief or hysteria whenever she wished. But his voice was not unkindly.

'Get some clothes for the night, Miss Grey, and what else you'll need,' he said.

She took no notice, and Bristow frowned.

'All right, Wilson. If she doesn't start packing in five minutes, telephone Mrs Vere. She'll come and do it for her.' Bristow went out, and as he did so was confronted by Mannering and Armitage.

Still red in the face, Armitage tackled him at once.

'Oh, there you are! Bristow, what the devil are you playing at? Haven't you the sense to see that the girl could not do anything like robbing her own mother?'

'I'm sorry, sir. I act on evidence, not sentiment.'

'Evidence my foot! What is it?'

'I can't disclose it,' said Bristow patiently. 'I assure you that Miss Grey will be well looked after.'

'It damned well looks like it!' shouted Armitage. 'You've nearly driven her to suicide as it is! What the blazes do you mean by frightening the life out of her?'

'Easy,' said Mannering quietly.

'Easy be damned!' Armitage shook Mannering's hand aside, and advanced on Bristow, his fists clenched and his manner threatening. 'Are you going to let that girl go, or – '

Mannering gripped his arm.

'That's enough, Tommy.'

'You keep out of this,' snapped Armitage, and he pushed Mannering roughly aside. He was trembling, and his face had turned a choleric red. 'Let's have this clear, Bristow. I – '

'It is quite clear.' Bristow's voice was sharp and incisive. 'You are interfering in a matter which does not concern you, Mr Armitage, and also interfering with the proper course of justice. I hope I don't need to tell you of the seriousness of that offence?'

Armitage, however, was now past common-sense. Before Mannering could stop him he lunged forward.

Bristow pushed him authoritatively aside. His eyes met Mannering's.

Mannering nodded, and Bristow turned to the stairs.

Armitage drew a deep breath.

'Go on, tell me I've been a bloody fool,' he muttered ungraciously, and without another word went heavily towards his own room. Mannering passed a hand across his forehead, more puzzled than ever by Armitage's temper, and yet relieved that a serious crisis had not developed. He was glad Bristow had taken the sensible course: there was a lot to like about Bristow.

Lady Usk's door opened.

'What – what was that noise about, Mr Mannering?'

'Tommy rather lost his temper, nothing worse.'

'Oh,' said Lady Usk. 'About Cecilie, I suppose. Won't you come in for a little confidential talk, Mr Mannering?'

Mannering eyed her with scarcely veiled dislike, noting that Cecilie's plight seemed to give her more pleasure than concern. Brusquely he said:

'I'm afraid there isn't time, Lady Usk.'

'Such a pity,' said Lady Usk. 'Well, if you must go, you must. If you see my husband you might tell him that I've a headache, and won't be down again.'

Too confused to think much about Lady Usk, Mannering hurried down the stairs. From the moment that Cecilie had whispered to him he had felt disquiet, almost alarm. He wondered whether Bristow had any idea that the jewels were in the girl's room, and if he had, whether he was leaving them there in order to trap an accomplice.

It was feasible, and even likely.

Mannering went in search of Lorna. She was coming out of his room, and turned back when she saw him. He did not like the sombre expression in her grey eyes.

'Well,' he said, 'here we are.'

She laughed, but without humour. 'And how I wish we weren't. Why do things always happen when you're about?'

Mannering shrugged. 'You can hardly blame me.'

She looked at him oddly. 'No. I suppose it's mean of me to mind how much you're enjoying it.'

Mannering kissed her. 'You know me too well, but if I can clear Cecilie and myself, it will be over for us. She put on an act for Bristow, of course,' he went on. 'All she ran down the stairs for was to tell me – ' he drew a big breath – 'that the jewels are in her room.'

'She admitted it?'

'And assured me she hadn't taken them. The room should be empty tonight. I imagine Bristow will send her to Winchester. If the jewels are to come out it will have to be *soon*.'

'John, if you're caught with them it's *finis*.'

'If it were the robbery alone I'd be inclined to let her take her chance,' Mannering said, 'but there's a connection between the robbery and the murder. I'm sure of it. Cecilie may have taken the stuff, but there's an accomplice. It might have been Woolf, but it could be the murderer – and that means any one of the people in the grounds tonight.'

'What a muddle the whole thing is!'

'Well, here's a theory that fits,' Mannering said. 'Cecilie and someone else stage the robbery, *or* someone here whom she knows well took them, and she afterwards discovered who. She gets them back, but wants to cover the thief. The thief is known also by Woolf, and while Cecilie's talking to Woolf the thief makes sure that he can't talk.'

'I can follow that,' Lorna said, 'but it's assuming so much. Why should she cover anyone?'

'No stranger than why should she steal them?'

'The value – '

'No, I boggle at that,' said Mannering decisively. 'She might have stolen them for revenge, even to give her stepmother a shock, but not to sell them for hard cash. I'll get them, anyhow – if I can.'

'John – you're not forgetting Cecilie could be trying to

147

get you caught? Remember that someone planted the paste necklace on you.'

'I'm forgetting nothing,' Mannering said. 'I must have proof of the thief before Logan talks. I won't risk Cecilie being found guilty if she isn't.'

'Although you know her room is probably being watched closely,' Lorna said slowly.

'I can't grant that,' said Mannering. 'Bristow's taken her away, and he'll search the room as a matter of course. When that's done he'll assume that the room's no longer of any use. Why should it be?'

'Are you more likely to find them than Bristow?'

'Yes.' Mannering slipped his hands into his pockets. 'Yes, I think so. Because I'll know they're there. That's always assuming that Bristow hasn't found them, of course. I think,' he added, 'that I'll have a talk with him.'

In his eyes Lorna saw a gleam that she had seen often before, saw a man who was less Mannering than the Baron. She knew that inwardly he was charged with excitement, that the risk he would take of getting into Cecilie's room and, if necessary, of handling the stolen jewels, was countered by the thrill he would get, by the old urge to be active – whether it was for, or against, the police did not matter. It was not wholly the need of blocking Logan's story which drove him on.

Chapter 19
The Jewels

It was dark in Mannering's room.

The luminous dial of his watch showed that it was two o'clock.

He had been asleep for a little over two hours, but the brief rest had done him good. In darkness, he dressed quickly, adding the rubber-soled shoes, and thin, cotton gloves. Except for the wind there was no sound. The storm had passed, and the air was cool and refreshing.

He twisted a dark scarf loosely about his neck, then slipped into a dark mackintosh and a wide-brimmed hat which he pulled down over his eyes.

He had no tools as the Baron had often used, but he had a many-bladed knife that would be useful with any recalcitrant catch, and a long, thin piece of wire which he could use as a pick-lock. They were amateur's tools, but used by the Baron they would be effective enough: he had no doubt of his ability to get where he wanted that night.

When he opened the door he saw a faint light in the passage outside, but there was no sound. He stepped through quickly, and glanced about him. No one was in sight until he reached the landing. Then, glancing over the balustrade, he saw one of Bristow's men sitting in the hall. On a chair next to the man was a heavy service revolver.

Mannering smiled, thinking of the days when he had outwitted the police and entered strong-rooms far more secure than Vere's was likely to be. In those days entering a room as he proposed to do now would have been no more than a minor incident. It would not be difficult now, unless Bristow had set a trap.

He reached Cecilie's room.

As he passed that of Lady Usk, he heard a confused murmur of voices. Usk's voice was recognisable but the words were lost. The argument he appeared to be having with his wife made noise enough to cover any sound Mannering caused, although it also prevented him from hearing others should they approach. He felt tense and yet full of confidence, for after he had left Lorna he had talked with Bristow – and learnt that he and Tring had already searched the room and found nothing.

Mannering turned the handle of the girl's door.

It was locked, and his heart beat faster. With the picklock it would take at most a minute – but every second he would be standing in the passage, in full view of anyone who glanced that way.

If his heart was beating fast, his fingers were steady enough as he slipped the wire into the keyhole. He stood tense and hardly moving, then the wire found purchase and the lock clicked back.

He turned the handle and stepped inside, closing the door behind him. The room was in complete darkness, and he waited for some seconds with bated breath. He heard nothing, no sound of breathing which he had feared.

He knew that each room door had two keys, and in the top drawer of the dressing-table he found the spare. He stepped to the window, unlocked the shutters, and pulled the window down. The air was cool against his cheeks.

After a few seconds he could see vaguely, by the light of the stars. It was a first floor window, and there was a long drop to the ground. He had examined the wall outside his own room carefully, however, and knew that a pipe with a granite surround led to the ground from the adjacent bathroom.

The layout here was the same. In an emergency he could get out that way. He shuttered the window and, satisfied that he had taken all possible precautions, he took a sheet from the bed and laid it across the bottom of the door, so that no gleam of light could get through.

He switched on the light, and looked about him.

He was looking for evidence of Bristow's activities, and that was not hard to find.

Mannering went about the room slowly. It seemed that there was nowhere Bristow had missed. Even the bathroom and hand-basin grids had been scraped, suggesting that Bristow had examined them to make sure nothing was hanging down the runway pipes.

But the jewels must be here, unless Cecilie had lied.

Mannering saw no reason why she should have done so, unless she had set a trap for him. He tried to forget that possibility, but it remained.

He was looking speculatively at the fireplace, when he heard the sound outside. It was dull but clear, and his heart turned over. He stepped to the door, but before he reached it he heard the sound again.

Bristow's man probably, patrolling the passages.

Mannering switched off the light, turned the key in the lock, and opened the door. Light filtered through, and the soft footsteps of a passer-by came more clearly. Mannering could see the back of the walker, and the somewhat stealthy posture.

As he reached the landing and turned towards the stairs, Mannering saw that it was Mike Deverell. But what on earth was Mike Deverell doing creeping about the passages during the night!

Mannering pushed the door to, but his heart was thumping lest Deverell had seen him.

The footsteps passed, on a return journey, and a moment later a door closed softly.

Mannering relocked Cecilie's door, and tried to concentrate on the search; but memory of Mike's furtive walk persisted. Automatically Mannering looked through drawers and wardrobe, but all the time he knew that the hiding-place – was somewhere far less obvious, somewhere in fact too clever for Cecilie to have discovered. That thought gave force to the idea that Cecilie was not working alone. Whether she had played a part in the murder of Woolf or not, it grew increasingly clear that there was someone else at the house with whom she was in contact.

Armitage?

Possibly. Mannering remembered that in the first few days of his visit Armitage and Cecilie had been on very friendly terms. Then Cecilie had professed to get bored with him, and Armitage had blamed the constant chaperonage of Lady Usk. Could the resultant coolness have been a deliberate effort to prove that they were *not* working together?

Cecilie's shouting as she had run down the stairs, her urgent whisper, were vivid in his mind. That had been less than five hours before, and from that time onwards she had been left alone. Had anyone else found the jewels?

Mannering looked towards the ceiling.

Two feet from it, along the walls, ran a picture rail.

Mannering pulled a chair to the wall, and carefully working his way round, ran a finger over the entire length.

On every part there was very slight dust – excepting a stretch of two feet or more immediately over the dressing-table. The rail was a wide one, and it *might* be hollow.

Mannering had forgotten Deverell, and everything but the search on hand. He examined the picture rail carefully, and he found what he was looking for – a slight break in the wood. Immediately above the dressing-table a piece some three feet long had been inserted.

Mannering felt a fierce excitement as he pulled gently at the inserted piece. He felt the wood move. There was a sharp grating sound, and a moment later it came away in his hand.

Beyond it was a cavity nearly a foot long!

Mannering found himself breathing quickly as he slipped his fingers into the cavity, and touched something beyond. He caught it between his fingers, and drew it out.

It was one of Lady Usk's brooches.

Another brooch, some earrings and a bracelet followed. He slipped jewel after jewel into his pocket, surprised at the capacity of the hole in the wall – and then his fingers touched cotton wool, and he pulled it out, feeling something hard wrapped within. A moment later he uncovered the necklace.

Mannering did not move immediately.

His expression was strained as he looked at the necklace, and then raised the shade of the lamp so that he could get the light to shine more directly on the diamonds. His breathing was shorter and a little laboured when he stepped down at last.

It *was* the genuine Deverell necklace: the diamonds were real.

*   *   *

A problem now faced Mannering.

Cecilie had told the truth, and the jewels, damning evidence against her, had been found in her room. If he handed them to the police it would condemn her. Keeping them from the police involved greater risk for himself, but he was less concerned with that than with the possibility that, if convicted, Cecilie would take the charge alone.

By leaving them he would be presenting Bristow with his wanted evidence, and lessening the force of Logan's story: but in his heart he knew that there was no question of letting the police have them.

Mannering slipped the necklace into his pocket, wrapped the other jewels in a handkerchief, and then replaced the strip of picture rail. When it was back he was surprised how well it fitted. Apart from a little dust, there was nothing to show that anything had been disturbed. With a handkerchief he wiped the dust away, and then he turned to the door. He knew that he would have to get rid of the jewels quickly: it would be disastrous if he were found with them on his person. The question was – where to hide them?

His eyes gleamed.

The obvious thing to do was to put them on Lady Usk's dressing-table, but apart from other complications, this would mean giving Lady Usk the real necklace for the false one.

He did not think there was any possibility that he had been mistaken in the first place, and that raised another problem. Had the fake necklace been planted on him deliberately, or had it been put there merely to withdraw

153

suspicion from the thief? And had Lady Usk also had the original?

He switched off the light and opened the door stealthily, then slipped into the passage. He needed to cross the landing to reach his own room, and he approached it cautiously but without suspecting that anyone would be in it.

He reached it – and then he had a shock which sent the colour from his face, set his heart thumping, and for a moment robbed him of the power of movement or speech. He could have sworn that there was no sound, but as he reached the end of the passage he found himself looking at Anderson, and he knew after that first split second of shock that the sergeant was as startled as he was himself.

The interval seemed to last for an age.

In it Mannering saw disaster ahead of him, knew that the jewels in his pocket would condemn him out of hand. The shock was so great that for a full five seconds he did not move. The sergeant recovered himself first. His right hand slid towards his pocket.

CHAPTER 20

More of Lady Usk

Mannering had little choice.

To draw back, to try to argue with or to outwit the man once the gun was in position would be fatal. If he were to be shot he could not help it. Injured or not, unless he outplayed Anderson now it meant complete disaster. With the one thought in his mind Mannering's right fist shot out as the man touched the trigger.

Anderson staggered back; but the gun went off. There was a roar like thunder as the revolver clattered to the floor. Mannering struck again, swiftly and savagely, sending Anderson thudding back against the wall.

Mannering ran past him.

He heard a shout from the hall, and footsteps rushing the stairs. A door banged from somewhere ahead of him, and another opened. As he moved he took the jewels from his pocket and flung them from him, not caring where they went in his relief that they were out of his possession. He ran on prepared to tackle whoever was coming out of the open door ahead.

And then he saw who it was.

'*Lorna!*'

'Quick!' she said. 'Get those clothes off.'

He swung into her room and she went out closing the door behind her. Mannering turned the key in the lock, and then stripping to singlet and trunks bundled his discarded clothes together. By then footsteps were hurrying past, and he heard Vere's voice, Diana's, and the acid tones of Hilda Markham.

There was a light tap on the door.

A jumble of voices reached his ears as he opened it, and Lorna slipped through, carrying his pyjamas and dressing gown. Under one arm she had his slippers. Her hair was tumbled, but her eyes were bright, and she looked excited rather than alarmed.

'Bless you!' said Mannering fervently. He slipped into the pyjamas and dressing-gown, ran a hand through his hair to make it tousled, and then put an arm about Lorna's shoulder.

'Bless you,' he said again.

'Bless me indeed,' said Lorna lightly, 'and thank heaven I wasn't asleep. Push those clothes into the wardrobe, we can get them back later. And you'd better make an appearance quickly, or Bristow will be after you.'

He said excitedly: 'Sweetheart, Cecilie didn't lie.'

'You found them?' For the first time she showed alarm. 'Where are they?'

'Out and about,' said Mannering. 'I threw them away.'

Lorna said: 'Well, that's something. At least I can provide an alibi if necessary.' She laughed as Mannering opened the door and slipped into the passage.

For a moment he thought that he was unseen, but he was wrong. Armitage, and Lord Usk were in sight.

Both men looked away.

As Mannering reached the landing he heard Bristow call sharply:

'Quiet please!'

Deverell was on the edge of the little crowd, and Mannering touched his shoulder.

'What's happened?' he whispered. 'More robbery?'

'I don't know yet,' said Deverell. Bristow looked up and caught Mannering's eye. There was a hostile, frostiness about the glance. Mannering's face was expressionless.

Bristow said quietly: 'I'm going to ask you all to go straight to the drawing-room, ladies and gentlemen, and wait there for a few minutes.'

Vere, Diana, Armitage, Usk, Hilda Markham, Lorna Dryden, and two of the secretaries, filed quietly past him.

When Deverell reached Bristow, he hesitated, then said tentatively:

'I heard a noise, or thought I did, not long ago, and came out to investigate.'

'Thank you, sir. I'll be glad of your statement later.'

Mannering was the last to reach Bristow. The Inspector said casually:

'A moment, Mr Mannering, please.'

'Of course,' Mannering regarded the Inspector sardonic-ally. 'What happened?'

'I don't know myself yet,' said Bristow sharply. 'You'd better come with me.'

'Manners, manners,' chided Mannering softly.

Bristow drew a deep breath.

'I'll be damned if – ' He caught Mannering's eye, then broke off and laughed. 'All right, you devil! Come with me, *please*.'

'Always glad to help,' said Mannering gently.

'Have you looked downstairs, Inspector?'

'I'm just about to do so, sir.'

'But surely Anderson was inside the strong-room?' Morency insisted.

'He was, but he found it too much for him. A mild form of claustrophobia, I expect. I had another man take his place after the first half-hour, and put Anderson on patrol. By the time we get back,' he said, 'he'll be able to talk.'

Morency nodded, and they hurried to the strong-room door. Tring was standing outside, his melancholy face showing no expression beyond a gloomy pessimism.

'Has there been any trouble here, Tring?' Bristow's voice was sharp.

'None, to my knowledge, sir.'

Morency turned impatiently towards the door. Bristow unlocked it. Beyond the second door they found a sleepy-eyed man sitting on a kitchen chair, gun in his hand.

'Everything all right, Wilson?' said Bristow.

'Yes, sir.'

Bristow turned to Morency. 'Do you wish to see the papers, sir?'

'No, that won't be necessary.' Morency, his anxiety set at rest, went off in search for his colleagues, while Bristow returned to the stricken Anderson.

The man still looked dazed, but he was on his feet. He said at once:

'I'm sorry, sir, but I was just too late.'

'All right,' said Bristow quietly. 'I don't suppose you let him go on purpose. What happened?'

Anderson explained: he had been patrolling, and had seen a man, fully-dressed, come along the passage. He had heard no sound of approach, and both of them had been startled. Then he had reached for his gun. At that point Anderson rubbed his chin ruefully.

'I'm afraid he got me first, sir.'

'Hmm,' said Bristow. 'Could you identify him?'

'No, sir,' said Anderson frankly. 'He was wearing a hat, and a scarf as a mask.'

Bristow said, almost casually: 'Are you quite sure, Anderson? Would he be about the build of Mr Mannering, for instance?'

So that was why Bristow had wanted him!

Mannering's heart turned over, but he forced himself to face Anderson.

'I think, sir,' the sergeant looked at him closely. He said slowly, 'that it was a shorter man than Mr Mannering. And he was fully dressed.'

'Thank you, Anderson.' Bristow showed neither disappointment nor surprise. 'You'd better get some rest. Oh, what way did he come?'

'Along that passage, sir.' Anderson pointed to the direction from which Mannering had come.

'You didn't see which way he went, I suppose?'

'No, sir.'

Bristow watched the man walking off, and then turned to Mannering. 'Well, Mannering – so you didn't take my advice.'

Mannering said evenly: 'I hope you're not going to start that again. You might remember that the man was fully dressed, and I'm not. I was here two minutes after the shot.'

Bristow shrugged. 'And it only needed two minutes to get rid of them.'

'I don't like your manner,' said Mannering sharply. 'It would be well to improve it. Someone broke in: that's obvious.'

'Obvious to whom?' said Bristow dryly. It was clear that he was convinced it was Mannering who had hit Anderson. 'We'll leave it for now. I wonder where –'

And then Bristow stopped.

He had been looking towards the hall, and Mannering saw his expression alter, saw a gleam in his eyes that was one of sheer disbelief. Then without a word he turned for the stairs and raced down.

Mannering stayed on the landing, leaning over the balustrade. He saw the diamond which Bristow had seen, saw Bristow pick it up, and then look about him.

'Do you want any help, Bill?'

'Yes,' said Bristow sharply. 'See if you can find any more of these.' He showed two diamond rings in his hands, and Mannering nodded and looked about the hall. It was Mannering who found the Deverell necklace behind a settee, and he called out sharply:

'Bill – this is your lucky day. Here's the star piece!'

Bristow stopped searching, and stepped towards Mannering. He picked up the necklace, his lips set tightly and his eyes hard, then he looked into Mannering's.

'My lucky day, did you say?'

'Well, isn't it?'

Bristow snapped: 'You know damned well it isn't. I wanted to find these where the Grey woman had put them. Now anyone in the blasted house might have taken them –' He broke off, then went on more calmly:

'Oh well, I might have expected it from you.'

'Bill, if –'

'Oh, don't try to blarney me!' snapped Bristow. 'I saw from the start that you didn't propose to leave this job alone. Understand this, Mannering. That woman robbed her stepmother, and afterwards arranged to keep Woolf in the light while someone else shot him. By helping her you're helping a murderer to escape – perhaps two murderers. Where did you find them?'

'Find what?' asked Mannering blankly.

Bristow turned on his heel.

Mannering called after him: 'Dare I point out that Lady Usk didn't hear anything – or apparently didn't?'

'You have proved that you will dare anything,' said Bristow testily. 'As it happens she took a sleeping draught after dinner.'

'Nevertheless,' said Mannering cheerfully, 'don't you think you ought to wake her? She'll be delighted to hear that her jewels are back.'

Bristow said evenly: 'If you like to take her the glad tidings, pray do so.'

Mannering shrugged and started slowly up the stairs. The elation of the moment had passed: he had outwitted Bristow, he had escaped when the danger had been so acute that for a few seconds he had believed himself finished. It was ungrateful not to feel more thankful.

He decided to look into Lady Usk's room. Mannering tapped on the door, received no answer, and tapped again. Still there was silence. He tried the handle, and the door opened easily.

Mannering stepped into the bedroom.

The woman was lying on her side, on one of the twin beds. Her face was half-buried in the pillow, and she was so still that Mannering decided not to disturb her.

For some seconds he stood almost equally motionless while all the time he felt his blood drumming through his ears, felt his heart beating faster.

Was it imagination? Or was there no sign at all of movement?

There was none: he was sure of it, and he stepped forward quickly, released from a paralysis that had kept him still. Gently he turned the coverlet back, saw the waxen whiteness of her face. He put a hand on her arm: the flesh was warm. He sought for the pulse, and there was no sign of life.

He hardly knew why it came as such a shock.

He had known that her life was threatened, had known of her fear, but to see her lying dead, beyond all hope, was too much to realise.

Peering more closely, he saw the faint bruises on her throat, saw the unmistakable signs that, despite the naturalness of her position, proclaimed that she had been strangled.

She had been dead before her husband had left the room, but Mannering had heard him quarrelling with her less than an hour before.

CHAPTER 21

Part of the Truth

Had Usk killed her?

Thoughts flashed fast upon each other in Mannering's mind. Of Usk's hatred towards his wife, the unexpected visit, the quarrel that had broken out within an hour of the peer's arrival. Mannering's suspicion that Usk had sent the threatening notes grew sharper, but no man in his senses would commit murder in this way, with the circumstantial evidence so strong against him.

Yet Usk would not know that a quarrel had been overheard in the early hours; and Mannering could not report it without rendering himself liable to dangerous questions.

There were other things.

Usk was an expert shot with a revolver: Woolf had been killed by a dead shot – and his wife had been frightened of Woolf. Was there a connection there? Could Woolf and Usk have been trying together or separately, to terrorise the woman? Woolf could have discovered enough against Usk to become dangerous enough to kill.

Mannering thought back. Lorna had told him that Usk had slipped out of the drawing-room a few minutes before the thunder. The peer could have gone straight to the grounds, killed the private detective and slipped back. The man who had escaped by car, still remained to be explained, but granting the premise that Usk had a motive for the first murder, other things fitted into place.

To be implicated in the major robbery, Usk would have needed an accomplice at Vere House, however. Cecilie might fill that bill, but judging from the evidence of the work on the picture rail in her room, Cecilie had been helped by someone else on the premises.

Someone else?

Mannering stepped away from the dead woman. In a dressing-table drawer there were a pair of loose gloves. He slipped them on. The safe was locked, but Usk's clothes were lying over a chair. Mannering ran through his pockets. He found a wallet, and in it a hotel bill. His breath quickened.

Usk, then, had been staying at the White Angel for the past two days, near enough to take part in the robbery!

With it was a typewritten letter addressed to Usk from the Woolf Inquiry Bureau. Mannering read with increasing tension:

My Lord,

In accordance with your wishes, Operator Logan will call to see you at the White Angel, Winchester, on September 20th, bringing with him a full report of her Ladyship's recent movements.

Yours respectfully,
B. A. Woolf,
Principal.

Mannering put the letter down and stared ahead of him. He could have heard, then, that she had been to the police about the loss. She had not been able to hide her fear that he should know; and her manner when she had staggered to the stairs had betrayed a fear little short of terror.

Mannering ran through the other contents of the wallet, but there was nothing more of interest barring a pencilled note on the back of a creased envelope.

See Wrexford, Thursday.

So Usk knew Wrexford – a man now under arrest on a charge of espionage. It involved Usk yet further, showing him to be connected with every angle of the mystery. Mannering saw Usk as both dangerous and ruthless.

Bristow *must* have these papers without loss of time.

He put them altogether in the wallet and stepped towards the bedroom. Not until then was he aware that he was being watched. For Usk stood there, and behind him was Logan pointing an automatic straight at Mannering.

Usk's lips were twisted, and his eyes were glittering as he spoke.

'Surely, Mr Mannering, you've learnt the dangers of being too curious?'

*　　　*　　　*

'Supposing you tell me what you're talking about?' Mannering found it hard to keep his voice steady as the two men came farther into the room, for the particular tone in which Usk had spoken, *was the one which Mannering had heard on the telephone at the White Angel, in the voice which had tried to warn Wrexford.*

'You should know,' Usk said. 'Logan caught you with the necklace, Mannering – not knowing Woolf had entered and put it there. You were proving awkward with your inquiries, and it presented an easy way to make you silent. But you followed Logan, didn't you? And you visited Wrexford and left him helpless for the police.'

'You're talking nonsense!' Mannering flashed.

'I think not,' said Usk. 'My dear wife had such faith in you, but you will regret that you tried to help her. You see, Mannering, she is dead – and you will be locked in the room with her. That will be very difficult for you to explain.'

Mannering was appalled by Usk's expression, by the savagery with which the peer's words were uttered; Usk seemed beside himself, as though things he had bottled up for years were coming out, almost against his will, as if he knew that this was no time for talk but could not keep the words back.

'It will be my word against yours,' he sneered, 'and under the circumstances yours is unlikely to be believed. Logan will not be here – he will leave the country when we have secured the papers. I will follow later. Those papers will yield ample profit, and I shall no longer need to live on *her*.' His eyes turned towards the dead woman, and there was cold hatred in them. 'I've made full preparations, Mannering, although your interference nearly upset them. That, and Woolf's obstinacy. Such a pity Woolf had a sense of patriotism. Had he been wise he would have been alive now.'

'So you've two murders on your conscience,' Mannering said.

'That doesn't worry me,' said Usk. 'I've planned to kill her for years. And as for your reputation for detection, that's taken a knock, hasn't it? You were so convinced of Cecilie's guilt.'

'You think so?' said Mannering. He counted his chances of escape as being negligible, nevertheless every minute Usk could be delayed *might* bring help. Such men were vain, he would play on that vanity. 'I could present some sound theories that might startle you,' he went on. 'For instance, you staged the robberies to keep the police away from the main motive – the papers. Yes?'

'Really,' said Usk. 'You improve.'

'You used Woolf and Logan, after you knew your wife was hiring them, and then you threw a scare into Woolf, but he disliked betraying his country.'

'Certainly you are right so far,' said Usk complacently. 'Once he learned what Wrexford was really after he tried to retreat, but earlier I had persuaded him to replace the real necklace with the fake. As you had the replica I had to put the real one back through Logan – Bristow would never have been satisfied with part of the haul. But Woolf was not loyal enough to risk his freedom, and he tried to make my wife help him, not knowing she could not. When it failed he insisted on meeting Cecilie. I encouraged that,' said Usk. 'It drew attention to Cecilie so conveniently. And Cecilie suspected Mr Armitage, and even tried to open his safe to find out. Logan put that to her,' said Usk smoothly. 'It gave the police their first suspicion, and then the evidence they needed so badly. Had you not chosen to visit her room tonight, and found the jewels where Logan had put them, the evidence that Cecilie was the thief would have been conclusive.'

'So you shot Woolf?' Mannering asked.

'He was so awkward,' Usk said. 'I had just time – and I was careful to have a man make off in a car to further confuse the issue. I then sent Cecilie a note that the jewels were in her room. She told you, of course, and you found them instead of Bristow. Very gallant of you, but a little unwise. I shall tell Bristow that I saw you coming out of her room before you met the policeman. I shall hint that my wife told me she knew the thief, and that will provide ample motive for her murder – by you,' said Usk suavely. 'It is most unlikely that Bristow will find out that it was *I* who sent the threats to my poor wife. I shall blame Woolf for that. It's most comprehensive, Mannering, don't you think? My word against yours – and the evidence on my side.'

Mannering said quietly: 'You are very confident Usk. Perhaps, too confident.' But he knew that the scheme Usk had outlined would damn him. He could see no loophole in it, no way of evading a charge of murder as well as robbery; and his mind was sick at the thought of the papers Usk was so confident he could get.

'A mastermind has the right to be confident,' Usk said sharply. 'And now I'm going to lock you in here, and take the key. You can shout as much as you like but you will rouse no one in the servants' quarters, and even if you do, they're locked up in their wing, Mannering, and I've a man guarding the doors.'

'You seem to have a lot of men,' Mannering said bleakly.

'I have enough,' said Usk. 'I've planned this carefully. I should not be wasting time talking to you but for the fact that the crisis has developed faster than I expected. I've had to send to Winchester for a locksmith – you would call him a burglar – who will get into the strong-room, you see. The police guards inside and outside have been looked after. They're in the drawing-room now – with the others.'

Mannering stiffened: 'Usk, only a bloody fool would try this with so many police about.' But there was an edge of despair in his heart.

'You think so? You don't know everything, Mannering. I sent to Defoe and Gresham and their secretaries and told them Bristow wanted them in the drawing-room. Everyone but the servants is in that room, the telephone is disconnected, the doors are locked and barricaded, and a car has been driven to the window to block it. There is just no way they can get out or raise an alarm, you see. And if you should say that there was a man in the strong-room let me disabuse you. There *was*. The police were attacked when they were relieving him. Bristow had the keys: he managed to throw them into the grounds when he realised what was happening. They're in the shrubbery and if I don't find them quickly my expert will be here within an hour. Most comprehensive, you see, Mannering. The strong-room is at my disposal. When it is over I, battered and perhaps bloody, will release the fools!'

Mannering felt sick.

There was nothing Usk had missed, nothing that was not explained; and there appeared no way of foiling the plan. He stared at the peer who was tightening the sash of his dressing-gown.

He said slowly: 'Usk, these papers are probably vital to the Allies. If they're lost – '

'They won't be lost!' snarled Usk, and the flame of hatred Mannering had seen in his eyes returned: he looked demonical, he raised a clenched fist and shook it furiously. 'They'll be sold where I want them to be sold! Don't whine to me about patriotism! I'd sell my soul to see England crushed. I'm *Irish*, Mannering. Centuries of oppressing the Irish have bred hatred. Logan hates your guts as much as I, the others are members of what you call the illegal I.R.A.!' He was trembling with hatred, with a passion that appalled.

At that moment the butt of Logan's gun descended with sickening force on the nape of Mannering's neck. His legs doubled under him and he fell without a cry. Logan and Usk slipped quickly out of the room.

The key turned sharply in the lock.

*　　*　　*

Mannering had no idea how long he had been unconscious.

He awakened with a splitting pain in his head and sickness in his stomach. The light was on, but it was painful to open his eyes. He straightened his legs slowly, and then memory began to creep back. Usk – the dead woman –

He remembered Usk's suave recapitulation of his preparations, the thoroughness of the plan to get documents of vital value. Mannering staggered to his feet, almost blinded by the pain in his head, and dragged himself to the bathroom. He ran cold water, dousing his face and head. The water was like ice on his throbbing forehead and temples.

One thought was going through his mind: he had to try to prevent the robbery. Usk had missed one important factor – *he did not know how easily Mannering could get out of the room without the key.*

The throbbing lessened, and gradually strength came back to his legs. His hands, too, were steadier as he sought, and found, a hairpin. This he straightened, and slowly inserted into the lock of the door. It was some seconds before the thin wire caught. More than a minute passed before the lock clicked back.

Gently he pulled the door open, widening it enough to see into the passage. In his heart there was a dread that Usk had left a guard; but no one was in sight.

He slipped into the passage.

Every movement was stealthy, calculated to maintain his steadiness as well as to raise no alarm, reaching the landing he stepped back swiftly to the side of the wall.

Footsteps sounded clearly from a nearby passage.

It was Usk, about to hurry down the stairs.

As he reached the hall, his voice came softly:

'Is Rossman here, Logan?'

'No, sorr,' Logan called. 'I just been on the phone – he'll be half-an-'our yet, and has sent the tools ahead of him.'

'It's work for an expert. We'll get outside and look for the keys,' Usk said sharply.

Mannering moved back to the landing, and looked down. He saw the drawing-room door heavily barricaded with furniture dragged from the dining-room. A muffled thudding came from within.

Mannering rounded the stairs: and then he drew back swiftly. Standing with his back to him was a thickset man with an automatic in his right hand. With infinite caution

Mannering retreated, watching the man carefully through the balustrade. Then, heedless of the throbbing in his head, he slipped the sash from his dressing-gown and made a loop with a slip-knot.

Waiting, watching for the exactly right moment, Mannering dropped the loop.

It fell plumb over the other's shoulders, and immediately the guard jerked his head up. This movement made it easier for the cord to slide about his neck, and Mannering pulled sharply. The noose tightened, strangling the cry of alarm in the other's throat.

The automatic clattered to the floor.

It did not go off, and Mannering felt relief, and hope. He tied the other end of the sash about the balustrade, then hurried down, and picked up the automatic.

A sharp blow with the butt was sufficient to render the guard unconscious. Mannering loosened the noose, eased him to the floor and then, pain stabbing across his head, dragged him out of sight of anyone who might pass.

Mannering was thinking:

The locksmith won't be here for twenty minutes, and they'll keep searching for the keys. If they don't find them I've twenty minutes – God, only twenty minutes!

CHAPTER 22

Full Understanding

Mannering, not daring to risk his victim coming round, tied the man's wrists and ankles with the sash, and stuffed a handkerchief into his mouth.

He slipped the automatic into his pocket, noticing that a key was in the ante-room door.

Farther along the passage he saw a small attaché case standing by the locked door.

He picked it up, tried the catch, and found that it was locked.

Forcing it open, he stared down at a complete burglar's outfit. These, then, must be the tools Logan had mentioned. Hardly daring to believe in his luck, he gave no more than a passing thought to the fact that Usk's cracksman had sent not only tools, but the high-explosive ahead of him. He was fully satisfied with the knowledge that he had everything he needed for the task at hand, although the nitro-glycerine would be dangerous and must only be used if all else failed.

He bent to the lock of the door, examining it intently.

He could see that it could not be forced, but must be cut out.

The wood-chisel was brought into use, and he used a rubber-headed hammer to drive it into the wood, making a series of dull thuds. He did not pause to listen; time was the vital factor. He cleared the chips away and restarted, hardly aware of his burning eyes and the dull pain in his head. He did not know how long he was working before the chisel went right through the wood. Quickly he drew it out, dropped it to the floor and inserted the saw. The oak was tough against the steel, but gradually the fine teeth made headway. He had the vertical piece cut, then one across piece, at the top. Three cuts were needed in all.

He was three-quarters of the way along the last when he took the hammer and struck heavily against the square block he had made by sawing. With a loud *crack!* the piece sagged. He struck four times, heavy, savage blows, before the block dropped to the other side, held only by the steel lock partly in the door-frame.

Mannering prised it away with the jemmy, then forced the bared lock back. He was leaning so heavily against the door that it swayed open, and he stumbled into the strong-room.

He straightened up, leaning weakly against the wall. Six safes in a row mocked at him. He dashed the sweat out of his eyes and approached the first, recognising the type and knowing that it would take ten minutes or more to get the one dummy door open; therefore each safe would take at least twenty minutes work to open completely. He returned for the nitro-glycerine, tight-lipped. No sound reached his ears.

Now he was conscious of the passing of time, knowing that he had been working for twenty minutes or more: Usk's 'locksmith' might arrive at any moment. With a chisel and hammer he was able to widen the keyholes until there was room for the phials of dynamite to stand erect.

Outside there was silence.

He placed the phials in gently, for there was enough in each to blow him to pieces if he dropped one and broke the glass, lodging them tightly but letting the fuses hang clear. He groped in his pocket for matches. A match flared, quivering in his hand.

He lit one fuse after the other, holding his breath as cordite fumes spluttered into his face: the first fuse was well down when the sixth was alight. He turned sharply, half-ran across the strong-room, and then put all his weight against the door. It swung to slowly, but each moment he was afraid the explosion would come too soon. If the door was not closed completely debris would crash through, and the noise would reach the men in the grounds.

It closed.

He leaned back, weak and trembling, as the explosion jarred him. The muffled roar was torture in his throbbing head. Another – a third. He pressed his hand against his ears and stood back as far as he could, until the sixth roar came. He gave himself no time for rest, knowing that Usk and the locksmith might by then be in the house.

He pushed open the door, and a billow of smoke met him. He fought against it, and when he could see, gulped at the sight of one safe standing almost intact. But debris from the others was all about the room, and on the floor an envelope was smouldering. Mannering picked it up, and emptied the other safes of all that was in them. There were four envelopes and half-a-dozen jewel cases; these he bundled into his pockets.

In the passage he wiped the tools he had used free of prints, ran the rag over the door, and then wrapped it about the butt of the automatic.

That done, he stepped cautiously out of the ante-room. As he went he tied a handkerchief about his mouth and chin, for if it were possible to prevent it, no one must recognise him. He was halfway up the stairs when he heard the front door open.

He reached the landing.

At that moment he heard Logan shout, and a split-second later the roar of a shot. A bullet hummed past him, followed by Usk's frenzied cry.

'*Get him! Get him!*'

Mannering reached the first passage, snatching the automatic from his pocket. A bullet struck against the wall, and plaster stung his cheeks. He saw Usk and Logan racing up the stairs.

Mannering fired three times in quick succession.

Usk staggered, threw his arms upwards, and then toppled backwards. Logan came on. A bullet cut through Mannering's sleeve, but he took aim carefully for Logan's legs.

The Irishman ducked –

He took the bullet in the chest, and Mannering saw an expression of pain and bewilderment on his face before he fell, thudding heaviiy against each stair.

Mannering stared towards the door.

The noise of the shooting must bring the others from outside, and he had only three bullets left. How many men would there be? Where were the guards inside the house? How could he get assistance – ?

And at the same time prevent the police from knowing that he had broken into the strong-room?

* * *

Mannering had a minute's respite.

Then he heard hurrying footsteps. He saw an armed man rushing from the servants' wing: the man reached the landing and stared down stupefied.

Mannering retreated quickly into a nearby room.

On the dressing-table were two heavy, silver-backed brushes. He whipped them up, and nipped back to his observation post. The front door stood open and two others came through.

Mannering threw a brush aiming at the first man who still stood on the landing. It struck him heavily enough to send him off his balance. He toppled over, while his gun dropped to the first stair. Mannering moved forward swiftly as the men in the hall stared upwards – and he saw that neither of them was armed!

His voice rasped: 'Stay right where you are!'

The men saw him and the gun in his hand, saw the gun held unwaveringly as Mannering stooped to retrieve the other.

The fallen man staggered to his feet, obeying the threat of Mannering's gun and joining the couple. Mannering kept his head lowered, with the handkerchief covering the lower part of his face. He went down with a gun in each hand, speaking roughly as he went:

'How many more of you?' A pause and then: '*How many?*'

'It's – the lot,' gasped one man.

'Which of you is Rossman?' snapped Mannering.

One of them took a shuffling step forward, sending relief through Mannering's mind. He had feared the 'locksmith' was still to come, perhaps with others. He realised that he had them all, could he handle them?

'Get to the strong-room,' he ordered sharply. 'Walk backwards, damn you!'

They obeyed. When they were far enough away for safety he pulled the door on them, and turned the key in the lock. The tools were inside but no man could open that door in less than twenty minutes. He stared at it for a moment and then he laughed. The laughter shook him helplessly and he did not stop until he heard a heavy thudding. He swung round with alarm, to realise it came from the drawing-room.

On his own he was helpless to shift the barricade, but that mattered little, the urgency was past.

He went unsteadily upstairs to Vere's study, glanced about him, and stepped to the desk. The middle drawer was unlocked but the key was in it. Mannering pushed the documents inside. One of them was singed, and through the partially burnt envelope Mannering read:

Plan of Economic and Financial Agreement
with U.S.A.
Prepared by Martin Vere, Esquire, and Miss
Hilda Markham
Urgent consideration by Exchequer

and in pencilled words beneath it:

Urgent. Arrange discussion with M'cy at V.
House – G.

Not until then did Mannering realise that copies of the statement must have been at Vere House all the time, before Morency or the others had arrived. The 'G' was Gresham, who had come to discuss Vere's plan *as well* as see Morency.

Small wonder that the Veres and Hilda had been jumpy, that they had appealed to him to help to find the 'petty thief' – who all the time had been searching for the statement, trying to hide his real motives by the pilfering.

Mannering pushed the jewel cases into the cabinet, then made his way to the servants' wing.

The swing door was locked, but he forced it with little

trouble. No one was on the other side; the shooting would not have penetrated so far. He went a little way along the passage to the stairs, and then fired a shot towards the ceiling.

As the report faded, he heard the opening of a door, and then Ransome's startled voice.

'Did you hear that?'

Another servant answered, but Mannering waited for nothing more. He went back swiftly to his room, to wash his blackened, unrecognisable face and hands.

That done he pushed the soiled towel into the wardrobe, and keeping the handkerchief about his face, went out. Five menservants and three women were in the hall, moving the furniture, and he smiled. He dropped the gunman's weapon to the floor of the landing, walked to Usk's room and went in. After a minute's careful manipulation he locked the door on himself. Keeping away from the bed, with its grim burden, he set himself to wait.

*　　*　　*

It was as well, reflected Chief Inspector Bristow, that the Chancellor and the others had been too relieved at the safety of the papers to insist on a thorough inquiry that night. There would be a formal investigation, of course, but officially there would be no full explanation. Bristow, tired but relieved of a great anxiety, smiled obscurely.

'Read Mr Mannering's statement again, Tring,' he said.

The sergeant obeyed. It included a verbatim statement of Usk's admissions, but finished where Usk and Logan had left the room. Logan was dead; Usk would recover but he was unlikely to talk; he was a fanatic and he would die one. But from sheer malevolence he would have named the man who had smashed his scheme had he been able to.

'All right,' Bristow said, and he cocked his eye towards the sergeant. 'He's a clever beggar, isn't he Tring?'

'And just as well he is, sir,' said Tring fervently.

'I won't disagree,' Bristow said. 'I'm going along to see him now.' He went out, fingering his moustache thoughtfully. He found Mannering lying in bed, with a bandage about his head. Lorna stood by the wardrobe, in her hand a blackened towel.

Bristow stared at the towel deliberately, and then turned to Mannering.

'This is another thing you won't admit,' he said, 'and another I won't forget. I've a feeling that you've done even more than you realise, Mannering.'

There was a bang on the door, and Armitage poked his bandaged head inside. He was clearly in a good humour.

'Ah, Bristow! What about Miss Grey?'

'She should be here at any time, sir,' said Bristow equably.

'Good,' said Armitage. 'Sorry I lost my head and all that, eh?' He grinned. 'Y'know, I was worried about Cecilie. By the way, who gave me that bang? Have you found out yet?'

'One of the gentry who didn't like your curiosity,' said Bristow grimly.

Armitage waved a hand towards the bed.

'Nice work all round, anyhow,' he said, grinning at Mannering. 'Have a day or two off, old man, you need it. An expert who gets knocked out and nearly framed for a murder ought to give up criminology altogether. Don't you agree, Inspector?'

He winked.